Core Memories

The Chronicles of Bryce & Erin

Brian Scala

Title: "Core Memories: The Chronicles of Bryce and Erin" / Brian Scala
Description: Paperback First Edition
Publication Date: September 17, 2024
Editing: Samantha Moran
Also available in eBook edition

"Dinner For Two" / Brian Scala
Publication Date: August 31, 2023
Editing and Formatting: Samantha Moran

"Sinful Peaks" / Brian Scala

Publication Date: November 23, 2023

Editing and Formatting: Samantha Moran

"Black Number One" / Brian Scala

Publication Date: January 25, 2024

Editing and Formatting: Samantha Moran

"The Unaliving" / Brian Scala

Publication Date: July 1, 2024

Editing: Samantha Moran

Contents

Note From The Author

Core Memories is intended for mature audiences only (18+). Please proceed with caution.

Some portions are told from the point of view of a character suffering from various mental health issues.

As a whole, this novel contains passages with strong language and content related to the following (in no particular order): sex, violence, masturbation, domestic violence, death, murder, serial murder, assault, oral sex, dubious consent, non-consent, mental illness, blood, terrorism, cancer, rape, and unprotected sex.

If any of the above topics are disturbing to you, you may not wish to continue with this text.

Thank you!

Core Memories Playlist

Want to listen to a playlist inspired by *Core Memories*? Feel free to scan this QR code and find it on YouTube.

Dedication & Author's Note

This story is dedicated to everyone who's ever thought to themselves, "That sounds great, but I can't do that." I literally said those words mere moments before finding my inspiration to write a spicy romance. Thus, you *can* do it.

This novel began as a one-off short story called "Dinner For Two," and was originally intended to be a series of spicy shorts. Over time, I realized the magnitude of the story unfolding before my very eyes. What began as a fun side project became a rich tale about second chances, complete with real character development.

There are two things to take away from the following text. It's never too late and you never know where the journey will lead you or what lies ahead.

Episode One: Dinner For Two

Bryce Palmieri rises from his aisle seat in 7C as the plane comes to a halt at Gate 231. Like cats trapped in a carrier for what seems like an eternity, the other passengers on Flight 1038 all scramble for a moment, then eagerly stand. Their bodies lie in wait, but their minds dart every which way, pausing impatiently for the crew to prepare for arrival.

This is an all-too-familiar routine for Bryce, the forty-four-year-old regional sales manager. The restaurant franchise his grandfather founded in 1969 has grown rampantly since making it out of the great recession of the late 2000's unscathed. The Mid-Atlantic institution has expanded its reach beyond its home base in Ashburn, Virginia, opening new locations as far north as Orono, Maine and as far south as Brunswick, Georgia.

Now, thanks to a grand vision by Mitch Irvine, CEO of Palmieri's, they have decided to tap into a new market. The company is throwing a Hail Mary they hope will be caught by the sunshine state. Mitch has conveniently disregarded the definition of regional. Who better to close the deal than the man whose company bears his name and his family's legacy?

Bryce finally marches down the aisle, off the plane and onto the jetway. What greets him on the other side is unfamiliar and stark. He has seemingly entered a new dimension. A cathedral disguised as an airport terminal overcomes his five senses.

Bryce is captivated by windows galore, light fantastic, and steel wonders and architecture most becoming of a modern engineering miracle. The experienced traveler soldiers on toward the ground transportation area where he will board a shuttle bus to pick up his rental car. Gone is that classic green pattern carpet, so iconic that local residents and frequent travelers have purchased airport-commissioned socks representing its likeness. Missing is that masterpiece of an atrium and the airport shuttles that were long considered the unofficial first ride of theme park enthusiasts.

There are no monorails, no disingenuous automated public address announcements from the mayor blaring over the loudspeakers. Bryce glances ahead and sees a few other unfortunate souls walking down the same endless, magnificently sterile corridor.

Stopping to sift through his short blonde hair, Bryce checks to see if he has somehow arrived at the wrong airport. Alas, a message on the arrival board confirms his destination. Bryce has indeed arrived in Orlando, Florida. The new Terminal C is the longest, most boring journey he has ever endured.

An hour later, Bryce checks in at the Crystal Palms Resort and Convention Center. Family-friendly theme park resorts aside, it is far and away the most luxurious hotel available to those traveling to Central Florida for business.

At this moment, the muscular, five-foot-ten divorcee is not interested in the pool, the fitness center, or taking in a quick nine holes at the Falcon Crest golf course. He is not even concerned with the score of the Nationals game back home. Spectrum TV can wait.

Bryce walks into the master bedroom in his suite and closes the door. More clean, generic furnishings surround him. Beige, stucco walls with white painted wooden doors separate his bedroom from the bathroom, complete with new shower door and fixtures. Laying in the center of his bed, he reaches into his pocket for his phone. It is three-thirty in the afternoon on a Saturday in August. Bryce clicks on his messenger app and finds his conversation thread with Erin Gillies. Her smiling profile photo always disarms him. He informs her of his arrival.

> Hi, Erin! I'm all checked in here in Orlando. Are you in town? Do you have some time to maybe meet up?

Bryce's mind races feverishly. His history with Erin plays out via random flashbacks in his head – those first encounters with her at Walker-Grant Middle School, his longing for her affections, his remarkable discovery years later that she had become a full-fledged flight attendant, albeit for little-known Swan Airlines.

Bryce reverts back to Earth Science class when he'd turned his head and inadvertently found Erin bent over, reaching for her fallen pen, the first three buttons on her red blouse conveniently open.

For all of his life's accomplishments, the vision of Erin's massive breasts bursting from her top remains a core memory for Bryce. His shyness faded as he became a young adult. However, all teenage Bryce could muster at the time was the occasional 'hello' and the dream of catching his new crush in a compromising position once again.

> Hi, Bryce! I'm actually stuck on an 18-hour layover in Myrtle Beach. I have plenty of down time, though. Wanna FaceTime?

While excited about the opportunity to talk with Erin in real time, Bryce is disappointed that he's traveled to her home base, only to find she is not there. He briefly composes himself and replies in the affirmative, offering his number to Erin.

Bryce adjusts his position along with the collar of his grey, short-sleeved fishing shirt. He sits upright near the edge of the bed. A few deep breaths later, that familiar ringtone lights him up. After one more calming exhale, he answers.

"Hi, Erin!"

"Heyyyy!" she replies in a faded southern accent.

The five-foot-eight Erin is seated at the foot of her hotel bed, grinning earnestly, makeup still intact, and her natural auburn hair still perfectly bunned. Unlike in most of her previous social media videos, a few freckles appear on her face.

"Ooooh, no soap opera filter," notices Bryce.

"Nope, you get the real deal, Holyfield!"

"Yes, I do," he answers. "Although, I was kinda hoping maybe I could get the real deal in the flesh."

"Yeah, well, you know how my schedule is," Erin says in resignation. "Plus, somebody called out sick last night and I had to take the morning flight to the Grand Strand. I'm stuck here on call until tomorrow."

"Hmmm, no deadheading back?" Bryce wonders.

"No, they moved somebody around to cover a flight from here to Charlotte," responds Erin. "I mean, I've long since given up trying to figure it all out. You know... small airline, budget issues... I'm sure you've noticed all the delays this summer. It's not fun right now, and I've got a couple more years until I can get my pension."

Bryce realizes the conversation is diverting into negativity and backtracks.

"Well, it's wonderful to see you, no matter what," he confirms.

"Thanks!"

"You're still in uniform," beams Bryce. "You know I love a lady in uniform."

"Yeah!" replies Erin. Her eyebrows raise in acknowledgement. She lifts her chest and stretches her right arm out to give Bryce a better view of herself in full regalia - a short navy-blue blazer with a color-coordinated scarf around her neck. Erin's matching knee-length skirt remains off camera. Her white shirt barely contains her 48DD's, which does not go unnoticed by Bryce. He unsuccessfully tries to hide his gasp.

"Mmmm, I thought you might appreciate that," Erin slyly offers. She then redirects the conversation so as not to get Bryce worked up too quickly.

"So, when's your meeting?" she asks.

"Uh, Monday," he answers. "Total waste of time if you ask me. I told them this is not exactly an untapped market. I mean, you know. It's not like there's a dearth of dining opportunities here."

"Oh, believe me. I know!" Erin confirms.

"You've seen Route 192. There's literally a restaurant every tenth of a mile."

Erin nods in agreement. "Tourist trap."

Bryce's smile slowly dissolves as he tries in vain to think of a smooth way to switch topics again. Nothing suitable comes to mind.

"So, was that your most requested video on your *fun* Instagram account?" he wonders. "The naughty flight attendant?"

Erin raises her eyebrows. Her Cheshire Cat grin and widening dimples answer Bryce before she can even speak the truth.

"Absolutely. That's everyone's favorite..." The object of Bryce's affections sits perfectly upright. The fabric on her white shirt stretches ever so slightly. Her buttons practically beg to be relieved of their duties. Erin's incredible breasts virtually plead for independence.

"But is it any real surprise?" she asks, rhetorically. "I mean, you said it yourself. *You* love a lady in uniform."

Bryce's breathing grows noticeably heavier. Shifting his weight off-camera, his eyes glance downward off-screen for half a second. Erin notices his lower body movements.

"Everything okay down there, Bryce?" Erin inquires in a noticeably deeper voice.

His eyes gleam. The tone in her delivery is like a light switch. Bryce instantly recognizes the tenor, the same phone-sex operator cadence that accompanies the many videos Erin offers to the masses. With the flick of her sultry, naughty voice, Bryce now knows where this conversation is heading.

Nonetheless, this feels different. This is not the typical fare. Twelve times before, Bryce had requested a custom video from Erin's alternate Instagram ego, "RedheadBombs407," and sent the usual fifty bucks in exchange for a one-minute themed roleplay. Her feminine wiles, coupled with her wild imagination and aforementioned curves, had satisfied him every time without fail. Even though Erin addressed him by name in each clip, it was only Memorex. *This* is live. *This* is here and now.

"Mr. Bryce, you're a good regional sales manager," Erin continues, her deepened suggestive voice still intact, smile bigger than ever. "I have a region you haven't quite explored yet."

Bryce can barely hold his phone upright. He cannot hide his shocked expressions. His body trembles as he tries desperately to play along.

"Miss Erin, I'm... always open to new opportunities," he replies, his voice cracking from nervousness.

Erin is unfazed by Bryce's response. Almost expecting his apprehensive reaction, she slowly removes her blazer and her scarf to reveal her unbuttoned collar. She proceeds with her own sales pitch, still committed to her bedroom tenor.

"I know all about supply and demand, Mister Bryce," advises Erin. She stares deeply into his eyes, her reflection prominently displayed on his phone. Erin unbuttons one more and immediately proceeds to undo the third, suddenly magnifying her cleavage. Her breasts drawing closer to freedom, Bryce slowly lays down on the bed in amazement.

"I have an untapped market here, Mister Bryce," Erin reveals. "Ready and willing to accept your terms... ready for a *grand... opening*!"

Bryce's nervousness fades as he makes a startling discovery. His eyes widen as his cock grows exponentially inside his blue khaki shorts.

"You're not wearing a bra!" he exclaims.

Erin playfully looks down at her chest, then peers back up at Bryce.

"Well, how about that?" she teases. "So, what do you think? Would you like to work with me on this project?"

Bryce cannot believe his eyes. "Oh my God, Erin! I'm so..."

Suddenly, the current live version of Erin encouraging Bryce entrances him. The vision of Erin's impressive cleavage triggers him. Bryce flashes back to that first week in eighth grade Earth Science class. He briefly recalls that thirteen-year-old girl he knew growing up in Fredericksburg, Virginia whose chest had unexpectedly blossomed over the previous summer vacation.

Bryce remembers sitting at those fixed wooden desks, simultaneously scared and amazed at his own wooden development. He had experimented with his own body as a burgeoning teenager. However, neither magazine photos nor ladies on cable television had made him this hard.

Bryce blinks and sees the woman she has become, so confident and voluptuous. Time has made her even more stunning and desirable. He wishes fate hadn't called Erin away from her home base. However, he will gladly take the ultimate live video experience with the ultimate woman as a consolation.

Bryce wants to say something poignant but draws a blank. He wants to forge ahead and make Erin feel the way he feels right now– so massive, so ready. With the rush of blood flowing into his lower head, Bryce can only muster the most basic of words.

"WOW!" he unconsciously mutters.

Realizing where his mind had gone, Erin barely stifles her laughter. She hasn't forgotten the awkward teenager he was all those years ago either, but that's not who she wants. She needs him to be the man he has become.

"Oh yes, Mister Bryce. You are a big man," she reminds him. "A *very*... big... MAN! That's right, MISTER Bryce! I need a big, hard MAN to help me make this very difficult decision... I need a MAN, Mister Bryce. I need *you, now*!"

Those two words – mister and man – echo in his brain while his cock throbs, hardening further. His expression suddenly shifts from anxious to certain as he regains his composure, remembering himself. A wry smile forms on his face as he focuses on his dual missions – satisfying both he and Erin as only a man can.

"Miss Erin, I can certainly help you," he answers. "But opening a restaurant is extremely... *hard*."

"Oh, yes. I know, Sir," she responds gleefully. "I'm willing to do *all* the work required of me."

Bryce sits back up on the edge of the bed and leans in. "Well, for starters, as you know, Orlando is quite hot and wet, especially this time of year. I don't know what kind of work attire you're considering, but you know what they say. *Less* is more."

Erin happily concurs. "Oh, yes. You're right, Mister Bryce. Maybe one more button will suffice--"

"Actually," he interrupts, his tone more demanding. "I was thinking of something a bit lower. I know you're wearing that short blue skirt. I don't like it. Not at all, Miss Erin!"

Erin's grin widens. Her chest heaves ever so slightly as her breathing becomes heavier.

"Oh!" she exclaims. "Well, I can fix that quite easily."

Bryce watches Erin place her phone on the nightstand and listens as she removes the offending piece of clothing. The incongruous image of the hotel ceiling is altered by the sight of her aforementioned skirt swaying back and forth over the lens. Erin tosses it onto the neighboring queen bed and picks up her phone.

Before showing her face once again, she pans down the length of her body to reveal the front of her maroon size twelve high-leg panties with lace trim.

"How's this, Mister Bryce?" she inquires furtively as she brings her Pixel back up to her face. "It's my favorite color."

"That's much better, Miss Erin," he confirms, his confidence growing to match the size of his erect eight-inch cock. "I like the way you think, which brings me to my next issue."

"What's that?"

"The menu," Bryce says. "Now, I'm sure you're wondering, 'How can we possibly alter basic Italian cuisine?' Well, you have something no one else does... Something I want!"

"Oh, and what might that be?" Erin asks.

"A juicy red snapper with my name on it," he answers as he tilts his head to the left. "I need to get a closer look."

With that, Bryce pauses and utters words he never thought he would say in a million years, not in any situation.

"Lose the panties."

Erin grins mightily. She props the phone upright against the lamp on the nightstand so Bryce can see everything. The flight attendant stands in front of the camera and removes her maroon underwear. She brings the lens in close to reveal a brighter shade of red, a landing strip that blankets her pink runway.

"I shaved for you!" she informs him. "It's just a garnish though. I think you'll find the main course is quite succulent."

A vision of Erin's pussy, coupled with the still-prevalent image of her breasts, overcomes Bryce.

"Oh my God, yes!" he exclaims. "Oh wow, Erin!"

No longer interested in playing the long game, Bryce pulls down his drawstring shorts and red patterned boxers, falling backwards onto the bed once again. His left hand is barely able to hold his phone to eye level as he strokes himself with his right hand.

"Oh, you like that, huh?!?" says Erin. "I knew you would, Mister Bryce, but... Wait, Mister Bryce!!"

Bryce's eyes and mouth widen, seeing his own imminent happy ending. Erin, sitting on the edge of her bed wearing nothing but her half-unbuttoned white shirt, grows despondent at the idea of Bryce finishing by himself.

"Sir! What are you going to serve *me*?" she asks intensely.

His massive cock now throbbing feverishly, Bryce barely hears Erin's fair inquiry.

"Oh, yeah. That's right," he answers as he slows his jerking motion.

"Yeah!" she replies with more than a hint of sarcasm. "I mean, this *is* dinner for two, is it not?"

Precum escapes Bryce's manhood, beading on the tip. He's halted his solo mission just in time. Smiling intently, Bryce's eyes apologize for his error. He centers his iPhone, looking Erin dead in the eyes.

"What would you like, Miss Erin?" he asks, still hard but with renewed commitment to completing their foreplay.

"Well, I hear Palmieri's has the BEST Italian sausage," she answers with conviction. "But I'm just not sure it's big enough to satisfy my hunger... May I please see it, Sir?"

Bryce is now the one who's barely able to stifle his laughter. "Ohhh, Miss Erin. I assure you. It's plenty big enough."

Lowering his left arm, he turns his phone to reveal his cock to Erin, smiling off-camera.

"Ohhhh! Wow!" she exclaims as she starts breathing heavily once again. "It's such a large serving, Sir."

"I believe in offering huge portions for our most valuable clients," advises Bryce.

Erin quivers in excitement. She shifts to rest her back against the plush pillows. Her eyes look over toward a mystery item, not visible to a waiting Bryce. Two seconds later, Erin emerges with a purple Classix Sweet Swirl.

"I think this is the same size as your sausage," she taunts as she turns on her vibrator. Erin quickly retrieves a clear acrylic book easel from the edge of the adjoining bed, places it in front of her, and rests her phone on it, enabling her to undo the remaining buttons on her shirt.

Bryce's body shakes as Erin's nipples greet him. His erection, never even close to fading since she'd popped her third button, feels larger than ten Washington Monuments. Inhaling and exhaling with the ferocity of a tiger, he barely has the presence of mind to calmly, softly seek permission to touch himself.

"Please... Miss Erin..."

She teasingly coos and tucks her people pleaser in between her massive breasts. The pulsating action catches Erin off-guard as she quakes uncontrollably.

"Ohhhh, Bryce!" she utters, inadvertently forgetting to address him as Mister. She squeezes her tits together, nearly hiding her pleasure toy completely between them.

"It's enormous, yet it disappears" says Erin in amazement. She arouses both herself and her favorite admirer by caressing her nipples in the process.

Bryce is almost in agony from anticipation of pleasure. He disregards playful prefixes and asks again, more intensely. "Please, Erin!"

Writhing in ecstasy, Erin gently nods. A most relieved Bryce exhales and grins from ear to ear, accepting his ultimate mission of climaxing with her.

"Ohhh, Erin!" he bellows as he resumes massaging his enlarged cock. "Oh, God, YES!"

Erin shifts gears, knowing they're both approaching the home stretch. She withdraws her vibrator from her cleavage and gently places it inside her wet pussy.

"Bryce!" she exclaims while quivering and rubbing her nipples once again with both hands. "Oh, God! It's finally happening... All these years, I've wanted you."

A stunned Bryce has nearly reached his limit. He mouths the word 'what,' but he can hardly wait to finish. Choosing to turn off his brain, he uses the right head to play along for the sake of the moment.

"You bent over for me on purpose, you bad girl," he declares. "You dropped your pen on purpose. You wanted me to see you, even then."

"YES!... Ohhh yes, baby!" reveals Erin. "I've wanted you for so long. And now... Ohhh, Bryce! Ohhhhh!!"

Bryce has nearly peaked, but his mind musters one final thought relating to food. "I almost forgot to tell you about dessert," he says.

Erin is about to burst all over the bed and cannot sustain anymore roleplay.

"CREEEAAAMMM... PIIIIEEE!!!" she shouts.

Bryce can no longer form words. The wet, nude, quivering woman of his dreams finally renders him incapable of anything but exploding in a blaze of glory. The sight and sound of her favorite restaurateur cumming is more than enough to make Erin, a notorious squirter, gush all over.

Bryce's labored breathing starts to subside. Typically, he would get up as soon as he was able to clean himself off. Instead, they both lay there, limp and ecstatic. It's a good twenty seconds before Bryce finally summons the strength to lean over and gaze into his phone.

"Hey!" he utters, as calm and relaxed as ever. The screen remains lifeless. The beige stucco of Erin's hotel ceiling stares back at him. No response.

"Hey, Erin?"

Bryce's demeanor dims considerably as he wonders when she will rejoin the conversation. A hand appears onscreen momentarily. Suddenly, the call is dropped. Erin is gone.

For a moment, Bryce feels the emptiness of loss. His emotions perplex him. Finally, he'd received something he wanted desperately from Erin, the closest thing he would get to an in-person encounter without her here. Yet, a numbness overtakes him.

Bryce harkens back to his college days and the heyday of chatroom cybersex. The few times he'd convinced some purported lady to partake, the ending was always the same. Bryce came and she went. The handful of times he tried NiteFlirt had left his body satisfied and his heart empty. Suddenly, he receives a PayPal notification on his phone.

You received a payment of $600.00 USD from Erin Gillies.

"What?!?" Bryce angrily shouts to no one. Furious, he grabs his phone with the intention of messaging Erin.

"Six hundred dollars?!?" he continues ranting out loud in an empty room. "You used me for—"

The regional sales manager of Palmieri's stops in his tracks. He understands the significance of the number – the total dollar amount he had previously paid Erin. Both he and Erin had gotten what they'd wanted all along. They both gave and received equally in time, money, and pleasure. In the end, nothing was lost and nothing was gained.

"It's a wash," he mutters to himself.

Bryce puts his phone on the nightstand, gets up from his bed, and saunters into the bathroom, taking a long, hot shower. As he absorbs the tremendous water pressure, he thinks about his meeting on Monday. Reconsidering going through the motions, he does his best to factor in the prologue and the promise of the sunshine state.

The Ashburn Village Center is plagued by rush hour traffic on the first Friday in December. Gloucester Parkway is practically backed up to Sterling, but neither holiday festivities nor rush hour traffic will stop Erin's brand-new Hyundai Kona from weaving in and out, racing to arrive by six.

For the first time in eight years, Erin is going on a first date. The last song she hears on her Spotify says it all. *Get it right the first time; that's the main thing.*

As fate would have it, Erin finds a spot directly in front of her destination with three minutes to spare. She parks and exits her vehicle. Erin is dressed to impress, not unlike her previous position. Her heels bump her up to an impressive five-foot ten, and she's donned a red blazer with matching skirt and a white dress shirt. This time, she wears a bra underneath.

On Monday, Erin will start her new job as Senior Analyst of Distribution and Strategy for Swan Airlines at their hub at Dulles International Airport. Tonight, she and her eHarmony companion are dining at a familiar Italian restaurant.

Erin enters the building with the confidence of a rock star. Dated picture frames featuring various celebrities of Italian descent line the walls in every visible room. Erin approaches the host, whose nametag reads Gina.

"Hi! Welcome to Palmieri's!" Gina greets her.

"Hi! Reservation for two?" counters Erin.

"Yes! Dinner for two... Name?"

"Garofalo," Erin replies.

Gina silently confirms the reservation. "Yes, I see that here. He has not arrived yet. Would you like to wait or be seated?"

"Be seated, please."

The host leads Erin into a dining area in the front corner of the restaurant, offering her guest an empty table by the window.

"First time here?" Gina asks.

"At this one, yes," Erin responds. "Just moved here."

"Very nice. Welcome to Virginia!"

Erin takes her seat facing the parking lot. A large, centered photo of Frank Sinatra presides over the room with a smaller photo of his suave colleague, Dino, strategically placed to the Chairman's right. Franco, the busboy, rushes over to fill her water glass.

"So, our specials tonight are veal piccata and Amore Special, a snapper with Italian sausage in alfredo sauce," Gina advises. "I know that sounds unusual, but I've tried it and it is absolutely delicious."

Erin cannot hide her laughter or the gleam in her eyes as she thinks back to that pleasure-filled day some four months prior.

"Oh, I've had that one before," Erin muses. "You're so right."

"Do you want to put that in now?" Gina asks. "It comes with a side of pasta, of course."

Erin unconsciously massages the outside of her full water glass and glances up toward the host. "I'll wait for my other party to arrive," she replies. "But I'll take the bottle of Pinot Grigio."

"Sure thing. Sam will be right with you."

Dino's dulcet tones echo gently throughout the room, reminding anyone within earshot that you're nobody until somebody loves you. Erin sits, legs crossed, and checks her social media accounts to bide her time. As the front door opens, Gina and her manager, Paulo, suddenly raise their arms with sheer delight.

"Hey, welcome back!" Paulo says.

Erin wonders who has garnered their attention. Curiously, she turns her head toward the entryway, hoping to see her tardy dinner date. However, in steps a familiar blonde bombshell, also dressed to the nines in a Versace La Greca Jacquard blazer with wide-leg matching pants and white embroidered shirt. An unmistakable presence.

"Bryce!" Erin softly exclaims.

Both he and Erin try unsuccessfully to stifle their joy and amazement. They have neither seen nor spoken since that orgasmic day. The sight of each other in person instantly rekindles their mutual desires. Erin slowly rises from her chair as Bryce smoothly approaches like a shark stalking its prey, ready to make another core memory.

Episode Two: Sinful Peaks

The abrupt slamming of doors in the adjacent unit awakens Erin Gillies from what feels like a thousand-year slumber. It had been the kind of sleep that momentarily erases one's memory for a few nerve-racking seconds.

Startled, Erin jolts and props herself into an upright position, momentarily frightened and curious as she struggles to recognize her surroundings. She looks around the room for anything that might jar her brain. To her left, Erin finds a marvelous, blonde-haired stud still sleeping on his side facing her.

Suddenly, everything comes back to her in one fell swoop, beginning with that unexpected first in-person encounter the night before, and followed by the drive back to his condo.

Erin beams as she recalls ripping each other's clothes off, both desperately wanting to experience the real thing, not a FaceTime fling. The memories of their fiery embraces and the intensity that never subsided vividly replay in her head. Her man had aggressively and forcibly thrown her into a frenzy, tossing her onto the bed, and fucking her in a cathartic culmination that was years in the making.

Just thinking about their lustful actions makes Erin wet all over again.

A smile almost as massive as the orgasm she had several hours earlier forms on the new Swan Airlines corporate mogul's lips. Her breath quickens at the mere sight of the object of her desire. Their impromptu sexy video chat some four months prior had been merely an appetizer. Last night, they devoured their main course.

Erin considers whether to leave him sleeping a little while longer or to wake him for dessert. After a second of contemplation, she decides to tempt sweet fate.

"Bryce," she whispers.

With sunlight on the horizon in Ashburn, Bryce Palmieri returns to the real world. Toned, shirtless, and immaculate, he slowly rolls onto his back and discovers his dream remains a reality. Not only is his fantasy woman still sitting beside him, but he finds another welcome development on this early Saturday morning.

"Well, good morning to you too, Mister Bryce," Erin says coolly as her gaze travels down below his mid-section. "It seems I still have your attention."

Bryce casually strokes his short hair, looks over towards Erin, and grins mightily. "Mmmm, you know I'm always happy to see you, Miss Erin," he remarks.

"I see!" Erin's eyes dart back and forth between his glorious face and the large peak under the comforter. "It's not cold enough to start a fire, but maybe we could start one anyway, like we did last night," Erin furtively suggests. "We've got plenty of wood for one."

Bryce calmly leans over towards Erin and touches her shoulder, sending shivers down her spine. Through the blinds, slats of the sunrise's light illuminate the pair. Bryce's eyes are like beacons. Erin's bra seemingly glows in the vanishing darkness of his bedroom.

"I was going to ask if you wanted to go to the diner," Bryce replies. "But perhaps we could have breakfast in bed instead."

Erin slowly reaches under the covers and smiles playfully. "You. Always thinking about food," she jests.

"I can't help it," Bryce answers as he shrugs. "It's what I do. I sell food."

Erin's right hand grazes Bryce's chiseled pecs and glides down his rock-hard abs. Her left hand follows suit, rubbing his nipple. His face cannot mask his mammoth delight as she proceeds to slip her fingers past his waistband and onto his erect cock.

"We had quite the feast last night," she reminds him. "Let's see what we have left over."

Bryce lays back and marvels at how Erin didn't even have to work to get him hard.

"Oh, wow... Yes!" he exclaims.

Fully invested, Erin's voice switches from a soft whisper to the assertive tone she regularly assumes in her roleplay videos. "Oh yeah, Mister Bryce," she coos. "That morning wood looks so good, so delicious. I could just *taste* it."

Erin moves her body onto Bryce, then shifts herself, hovering over his beltline. She pulls down his grey athletic shorts and pauses. With mischievous intentions, Erin whips them off Bryce's ankles and tosses them over her shoulder. She arches her back and corrals his thighs.

Bryce's breaths grow feverish. He now knows what's coming, and better yet, who.

"We won't even need coffee, Sir," Erin declares, her face inching ever closer to Bryce's swollen eight inches. "We have plenty of rocket fuel right here."

Bryce gasps and submits to Erin's will as she swallows his shaft. Spreading her legs apart, she strategically places them under his ankles, rendering him incapable of escaping from oral pleasure.

Alternating her rhythm between fast and slow, Erin uses the two speeds to tease him. After licking away his precum, she puckers her lips and momentarily lifts her head. Their gazes meet, Erin's emerald eyes commanding him to watch as she strips.

"No buttons to tease you with this time," she states as she laughs impishly.

Erin reaches behind her back, unhooks her bra, and releases her massive 48DDs. Voluptuous, bouncing, and heavenly, they cause Bryce's eyes to widen in sheer delight. He lifts his head, wanting desperately to massage her perky pink nipples and bury his face in her cleavage.

Struggling to release himself from her clever restraint, Bryce reaches for Erin's breasts. Quickly, she cuts him off, snatching his wrists and pinning them down against his king-size mattress as well.

"Oh, no no no!" she taunts. "You're not going anywhere until I'm finished with you. Or, should I say, until *you're* finished."

Strands of Erin's auburn hair fall in front of her face. Her wide, devilish grin leaves Bryce ecstatic. He'd seen that look of sensuality many times before in the videos he'd commissioned for his own personal satisfaction.

"You had your way with me last night, Mister Bryce," she reminds him. "You were so assertive! Now, it's *my* turn."

The calm way Erin reveals her master plan alone is enough to make Bryce's manhood throb. The tables have turned. His prey has become the hunter, transforming into a dominant force of nature before his very eyes. He has become the hunted, ensnared by her determination.

All he can do is muster a gentle, "Oh my God," and let Erin have her way with him.

Knowing his immeasurable desire to cum, Erin again takes Bryce's member between her lips and sucks him while holding down his wrists. Unexpectedly, she lowers her mouth and licks his balls, eliciting a spirited groan from the otherwise powerless Bryce. Her eyes widen as she playfully nips at the base of his erection.

Bryce moans loudly, knowing he is at the mercy of a woman who will show none until he is completely drained. He loses himself to the sensation. Erin continues sucking Bryce's shaft, provoking soft whimpers with each stroke. She asserts herself even more by deviously yet gently scraping his penis with her teeth. Bryce shakes and calls out with much fervor, which surprises Erin.

"Oooooh, caught you by surprise there, Mister Bryce!" she says through restrained laughter. "I can tell you're not long for *this* game... Well, actually, you are plenty long."

Erin pauses to fiendishly lick her lips and whip her red hair back. Knowing she has correctly assessed his lack of sustainability, Bryce's breathing becomes labored.

"Oh, Erin!" he shouts.

She beams like a villain, moments away from defeating her arch nemesis. "First of all, it's *Miss* Erin. I gave you a pass the last time you forgot that. Not this time."

Switching positions, Erin straddles Bryce, sitting upright. She resumes her missive in her typical bedroom tenor.

"You know, I just read an erotic short story where the reader could choose their own ending," she says. "So, I'm giving you a choice, *Mister* Bryce! How do you wish to meet your maker? I could suck you off, which will end you rather quickly, OR..."

Erin leans over Bryce's still-hard hammer, tits swaying above it. Unceremoniously, she grabs his manhood and shoves it deep into her vast cleavage.

"I could give you a nice, big titty fuck," she declares with a wicked gleam in her emerald eyes. "Which will end you, well, even quicker."

In awe of every stunning curve, and unable to hide his excitement, Bryce nearly ejaculates right then and there.

"YES! YES, MISS ERIN!" he yells.

"Oh, you remembered to call me Miss," she slyly responds. "I'm quite pleased, and I sure do remember how much you love my enormous, sinful peaks."

"Oh, yes, Miss Erin! Please!"

"Ah, there's the Bryce I know," she replies. "Hot, hard, and begging me to make him cum."

Erin leans over him and presses her elbows down into the bed, then squeezes her biceps into her breasts, burying Bryce's cock deep inside her cleavage. Though it would be easier to allow Bryce to mount Erin for his chosen finale, she won't relinquish control. She knows all it will take are a few well-executed thrusts to complete her mission.

Sure enough, the motions that follow are short and glorious. Bryce's animated bellowing increases in volume before he inevitably trembles and bursts all over Erin's chest.

"OHHH WOW! Miss Erin..."

With his last ounce of strength, Bryce watches as his cum coats her skin and drips down her belly. As his body collapses, Erin rolls over, examines the collateral damage on her breasts, and genuinely smiles. Bryce is rendered motionless, every inch of his mind and body in seventh heaven.

"Well, I'm sure there's another food reference in there somewhere," Erin remarks.

Unable to lift his head, Bryce barely summons the ability to respond. In little more than a whisper, he answers, "Cream pie."

They both laugh at the obvious callback to that night months ago. Once the levity breaks, Erin gets off the bed and faces Bryce.

"Washcloth?" she inquires.

Still giddy, he replies, "Hall closet. Middle shelf on the left."

A topless Erin powerwalks down the hall, finds two washcloths, and proceeds into the bathroom to do her business and clean off. The sound of running water encourages a nude Bryce to rise from his bed and follow suit.

Once clean and refreshed, Bryce and Erin return to the scene of their pleasures to retrieve their respective garments. He sits on the bed, wearing his shorts but nothing else, with his back against the headboard.

Bryce waits for her to fully dress and considers leaving well enough alone. Instead, with newfound determination, he asks one glaring, unanswered question.

"So, we never really spoke last night," Bryce points out. "I noticed you weren't wearing your uniform. Are you here for business or pleasure?"

Erin smirks and chuckles at the obvious omission. She sits on the edge of the bed by the footboard and raises her eyebrows before responding. "I think we've pretty much covered the pleasure part, don't you?"

"Well, yeah, I'd say so," Bryce replies with a wry smile. "Except mouth kissing. Funny how we both skipped right over that and got to the good stuff."

Erin giggles enthusiastically. "I guess that makes me the pretty woman, huh?" she muses.

"Are you against that sort of thing, like she was?" he wonders.

"Um, not necessarily," she answers with a teasing shrug. "But you're right. We never really said much after the day you came to Orlando."

"The day I came *in* Orlando."

Erin and Bryce both laugh heartily. "Yes, that too," she remarks. "Mind in the gutter."

Bryce serenely shakes his head. "I think we've established where both of our minds are, as well as our bodies," he remarks.

Erin sighs and veers the conversation back on track. "Well, short version for now. I accepted a new position with the airline," she states. "I'm not flying anymore. I'm in corporate, working out of Dulles."

Bryce perks up and pushes himself away from the headboard. "You're here now?"

"I'm here," Erin confirms.

Momentarily, his heart flutters and races at the revelation. Bryce rubs his face from top to bottom, then massages his hands. After a few seconds of seemingly uncomfortable silence, Bryce opts to clarify his position.

"So, I never really explained my situation," he says. "All this time we've known each other, it's never really come up."

"Well, I know you're single from your Facebook page," remarks Erin with a cunning grin. "I mean, not that it really matters."

"I suppose it doesn't," he continues, stone-faced and calm. "But for the record, I have no situation... and I don't want one."

"Any particular reason?" she asks.

"Well..." Bryce hesitates to answer. Deciding to allow a hint of vulnerability, he opens up slightly. "Let's just say once you meet the right person, they somehow turn into the wrong person. I've been in a few relationships. It's like once you become an item, the fun ends and the stress begins. That's not for me."

Erin stares at the earnest Bryce, honored and pleased by his admission.

"Well, Mister Bryce, let's add that to the list of things we both agree on," she replies.

"Yeah, it's a gradual thing, you know?" he continues. "One day, you wake up and the one you love, or the one you *think* you love, isn't there anymore. Before you know it, you find out she's a cold-hearted snake. Or worse, you find out she's married."

"Been there, done that, Sir!" Erin heartily responds. "Been on the wrong end of that one. But yeah, I decided long ago that kind of life wasn't for me. That's why I became a flight attendant."

"Always on the move," Bryce points out. "Never in one place long enough to settle down for anything... or anyone."

Erin decisively nods. "Yup, and I don't want that to change now. I took the job because I was tired of flying all the time. It's a major promotion and a huge opportunity for me, but I'm still not looking to settle down."

Bryce watches Erin as she pantomimes with her hands to clarify her next statement. "I wanted the job and I want *this*. I want what we did last night and this morning, which was amazing, by the way... But I don't want... *that*."

"Well, I don't want that either," he deadpans. "But this new position just happens to be here in Virginia."

"Yeah, that was a happy little accident," explains Erin. "Dulles is Swan's primary hub. I've been here many times over the years. I mean, let's face it. You saw me on that flight a couple of years ago and that's when this whole thing started."

"Right?"

"So, if I had worked for someone else based out of, say, New York or Chicago, we may never have reconnected in the first place."

"Fair point," he replies. "I never would have rediscovered that body made for sin."

"Oh, Sir," Erin furtively answers. "I've had this body for a long time, as you well know."

Bryce's curiosity overwhelms him. "That day in Earth Science, was that the first time you knew that you had what men wanted?"

"Well, it's funny because someone else just recently asked me that same thing," she says.

"Really?" he wonders. "Who might that be?"

Erin leans in and wickedly smiles. "Oh, just a friend."

"Let me guess. Another one of your, uh, gentleman callers?" Bryce retorts, then laughs and playfully looks away.

"Perhaps," admits Erin. "But getting back to your question, quick story and then I've gotta run."

"Alright."

Erin turns towards Bryce. "So, my father used to go hiking," she recalls. "He loved this one particular spot over in Strasburg called Signal Knob. It's about an hour away from our old hometown."

"Mmmm, I know that place," Bryce answers.

"Right. So, one day I told him I wanted to try out for cross country," she continues. "He said, 'Well, first of all, you don't have the body for it.' I didn't know what he meant at the time. I was about thirteen. Then he said, 'And second, you need to build your stamina.' So, we went to this trail over by Massanutten Mountain."

"It's lovely out there, isn't it?" he says, straight-faced.

Erin adjusts the collar of her shirt. She gets up from the bed to grab her red blazer from Bryce's closet.

"Oh, yeah! Magnificent" she agrees. "The hike is about four and a half miles long. I was totally oblivious as a teenager. I wore this pink spandex outfit. My dad looked at me like I had three heads. He just said, 'Okay, let's go.' So, I kept pace and I did the whole trail, but every man who saw me along the way did this weird double take."

"Because of the pink spandex," assumes Bryce.

"Nope. Because I was packing heat in my bra," clarifies Erin.

"Ahhhh!"

"Yep, bombs away, which is where the 'RedheadBombs407' Insta-gram handle comes from," Erin advises. "Trust me, no sports bra can hide these mammoth mammaries, anyway. Not then and not now."

Bryce slyly grins and shifts towards Erin, his energy replenished.

"Don't get too comfortable," she playfully warns. "I have things to do at my new apartment before I start this job… But, let me ask you the same question, Mister Bryce. When did you realize you were this super-hot sex god?"

Unable to hide his flattery, Bryce briefly lets down his guard and unleashes a light-hearted laugh. He slaps his kneecap.

"Well, if I must go down that rabbit hole, as you know, I didn't really develop my confidence until after high school," he reminds her. "So, I guess it was towards the end of my freshman year at Richmond. I mean, obviously, I went for Business Administration, but I played a little ball, too."

"Oh, really?"

"Yup," confirms Bryce as he looks up towards the ceiling to recall the exact sequence of events. "Played third base for the Spiders. I had a buddy on the team who had a girlfriend. She came to all the games, all the practices. Then, one day she wasn't there. I guess it was a week later when I saw her again. I thought she was there to see Bobby. I didn't think anything of it."

"Uh-huh."

"Well, this girl, I mean, she looked amazing," Bryce continues. "Amazing to me, anyway. She approached me and asked if we could compare notes from Economics. She was in my class, so we went back to my dorm. We were alone at the time."

Erin's smile grows as she listens to Bryce's retelling. Unconsciously, she begins rubbing her left thigh, which he notices right away.

"So, I told her I had to take a shower after practice," says Bryce with a twinkle in his eye. "She just started taking off my shirt. I was drenched in sweat. She didn't care... I mean, we just did it right then and there."

Now aware of her enthusiasm, Erin rubs her right thigh, too. In her mind, she pictures herself in the same position as Bryce's freshman-year lover.

"So, yeah, that was the first time I knew I could have anyone I wanted, Miss Erin," he concludes while staring her down.

"I'm sure you made her very happy," she dreamily replies.

"Yeah, I didn't make Bobby very happy," he recalls. "When he found out I was boning his girl, he threw a baseball at my head on the practice field."

"Fuck!"

"Yeah, we scrapped for a few seconds before the rest of the guys broke it up," says Bryce. "They kicked him off the team. I got the girl, at least for a little while. I'd say I won that fight pretty handily."

"Hmmm, I can imagine you are pretty good with your hands, Mister Bryce," Erin suggests. She suddenly rebounds with another key inquiry. "Oh, silly question... Did you know I was going to be at Palmieri's last night?"

A full-bodied laugh overtakes Bryce, who tilts his head before responding. "Nope. I live here and I work here. I go to that restaurant about once a week, sometimes more. The manager knows me by name. Truth be told, I was just as surprised to see you as you were to see me."

Erin looks towards Bryce and grins wantonly. "Fair point, Mister Bryce. Quite the fortuitous development. Almost as fortuitous as me waking up to your morning wood."

Bryce chuckles and slowly stands. Like a phoenix rising from the ashes, he stalks over to her, motioning towards his crotch. "Well, Miss Erin, that's not luck. I assure you."

Erin unsuccessfully tries to hide her gasp. Last night's sexual encounter still lingers in her mind and reverberates throughout her body. Desire rapidly overtaking her, she anticipates one last round of sensual release, but not before a final question.

"So, now that we're both here in the flesh, does this mean you no longer need to see my videos?"

Bryce hovers over Erin. His facial expressions transform from that of defeated prey to the cerebral assassin he was mere hours earlier. He steps forward, placing his legs between hers. His eyes zero in on his target. Erin's body quivers once again as she gazes up at him.

"Oh, I still want your videos, Miss Erin," he states with total conviction. "But I lied to you. There *is* something else I want."

Before Erin can ask what Bryce desires, he leans in and kisses her firmly on the lips. Gently, he collapses on top of her, letting Erin wrap her hands around the back of his neck. The vigor of their embrace snaps the third button on her white blouse, sending it flying across the room.

Startled and amazed, Erin's eyes bulge as she holds Bryce's head up, trying desperately not to cackle like a teenager.

"Oh my God, Bryce!" she exclaims, inadvertently forgetting to call him Mister. "Something tells me that's not exactly what you were trying to do."

Unable to keep a straight face in the heat of the moment, Bryce temporarily loses his focus. "I finally got to see those buttons pop after all these years."

Erin loses her resolve and laughs mightily. The two passion-hungry companions let the moment breathe as their foreheads touch. For a few seconds, Erin wonders if this was the fate that she and Bryce both swore minutes earlier they would never pursue. Erin's heart pulses exceedingly fast as flashbacks replay in her mind. She briefly relives every intensely fulfilling bedroom moment with the few men she dared to call her significant other.

Just as swiftly, she recognizes how every one of those instances led to despair. Erin refocuses her energy on the here and now and reminds herself that sex is her primary objective.

Bryce regains his composure, his swagger, and his bedroom voice. He arches his neck to allow a few inches of space between himself and Erin.

"That was a happy little accident, too," he says. "But that's not what I was looking for either. Furthermore, Miss Erin, you did not address me properly."

Before she can process his lecture, Bryce immediately slides down the length of Erin's body. With speed and precision, he shifts his head in between her legs, then shoves his left hand under her crotch panel and into her pussy.

"OHHH, BR...OHHH, Mister Bryce!" Erin screams with sheer delight, gasping for air.

Before Erin can catch the breath Bryce stole from her, he swiftly reaches underneath her ass and pulls her panties off. She tries in vain not to grin from ear to ear, but she cannot contain her excitement in any way, shape, or form. Though she has been in this position many times over, never has she experienced oral stimulation from him, the man who gives her the most pleasure.

Erin lays across Bryce's bed, ready and waiting, fully clothed except for her underwear and a wayward button. She waits for her man to enjoy the meal he offered upon their awakening.

Like a bolt of lightning, Bryce's tongue dives deep inside Erin repeatedly, inciting her to moan wildly like she never has before.

"Holy fuck! Ohhhh, Mister... Ohhhh!" she bellows.

Erin's body trembles and throbs. She knows she is in the presence of a man who is aware of what he is doing, who knows how to find every spot and make her uncontrollably wet.

Bryce's relentless pursuit of Erin's orgasm has no limits. His hands push up her red skirt, deftly caressing her legs. His warm palms press against her sides. The sensation of his biceps brushing against Erin's thighs overwhelms her.

Bryce's tongue continues to massage Erin's pussy, enjoying every delicious inch of her. A subtle "Mmmm" echoes throughout her body, causing her to violently pound the bed with her hands. His pulsating rhythm, along with his soft vocal stimulation, rapidly overcome her.

Erin flails briefly before clawing the comforter on both sides. Her eyes widen and her mouth falls, amazed at Bryce's oral abilities, and ecstatic that she's on the verge of cumming, yet somehow disappointed that he has mastered her vagina in record time.

"Oh My God!!" she yells. "Wow!! OHHH MISTER BRYCE!!"

Sensing Erin is nearly finished, Bryce makes one final push. With his joy buried deep inside her, she jolts and shakes vociferously. Like the midday summer storms that plagued Erin's former home base, her skies suddenly open and rain down on Bryce. Erin's climactic yell booms throughout the Winged Eagle condominium complex.

Bryce slowly and excitedly rises from underneath Erin. His face drenched in pleasure, he quietly retreats to the bathroom to wash himself off. When he returns to Erin's side, she is still motionless, recovering from the explosion. Her breathing gradually returns to a normal pace. Bryce smoothly lays down beside her, props his head up with his arm, and waits for Erin to move once more.

Erin places her hands at her sides and rolls over to meet his eyes, her dimpled smile one of complete satisfaction.

"By any chance, was that what you wanted?" she teases.

Bryce laughs boisterously and slaps his thigh. "I was still hoping to offer you breakfast, but I think I'm full for now."

Erin raises her eyebrows and chuckles. "I told you I squirt."

Bryce nonchalantly sits up on the edge of the bed. Locating Erin's discarded black underwear, he fetches them from across the room. Erin cackles, attempting to regain her composure, then gets up and touches Bryce's cheek.

"I *really* should be going," Erin says as Bryce hands over her panties. "I have some big weekend plans."

Slowly, she stands, trying unsuccessfully to hide her momentary dizziness.

"Whoa! That hasn't happened in a while," she notes.

After regaining her footing, Erin walks out of Bryce's bedroom and down the hallway. She does not look back. She knows he's following her to get one last look. It's only when Bryce's dream girl reaches his front door that she turns towards him. Despite feeling his presence, the burning stare of the statuesque Bryce catches her off-guard.

"This is turning into a Midwestern Goodbye, Sir," she sarcastically offers. "We've done everything, haven't we?"

Stoic and undeterred, Bryce asks his favorite lady one last question.

"When will I see you again?"

"When will we share sinful moments?" Erin asks, voice full of humor.

"Exactly."

Erin sighs and does her best not to melt. Last evening and this early morning have gone above and beyond her expectations. However, she will not allow herself to completely give in.

"That is entirely up to you, Mister Bryce," she says. "Tell you what, though. Check your Instagram later this weekend. There might be a special message just for you."

Bryce stands there, shirtless, hands in his pockets, his smile seemingly affixed for good. He considers a goodbye kiss but slowly backs up, also not wanting to dissolve his self-imposed boundaries.

"You got it, Miss Erin."

Bryce's fantasy-lover-turned-reality exits the condo. He does not watch her walk to her car, sensing she is fine. Despite his steadfast refusal to be more than casual sex partners, he wonders how he can top the past twelve hours with Erin.

"Just like last time... Core memory," he mutters.

As the sun rises and shines down through the northern Virginia sky, Bryce walks back towards the bedroom to ponder what comes next. As if the universe had read his mind, he suddenly receives a text on his phone.

A wry smile forms on Bryce's face as he briefly contemplates his answer. After a subtle nod of self-approval, he writes back.

Bryce sighs and rationalizes that planning more dirty deeds is preferable to coming down from this all-time high. "The next best thing," he softly reveals aloud as he receives confirmation.

Yours.

He stops by the bathroom and decides on a shower before beginning the day. Turning on the faucet, he drops his shorts on the floor, steps inside, and allows the water to cleanse his body.

Erin is determined to revisit her past accomplishments the following morning. She leaves her new home in Sterling before dawn to travel sixty miles west into the Shenandoah Valley. An hour later, she takes the exit ramp off I-81 south onto Route 11. As she approaches her nearby destination, the Strasburg Diner that used to be a Denny's, she distinctly recalls the words her proud father had spoken when she conquered his favorite hiking trail.

See those mountains over there? You did that. Don't ever let anyone ever tell you it's not possible. You hit a grand slam, now let's go eat one.

Sunrise is imminent on this cold, November Sunday. The diner has just opened for breakfast, and one lonely vehicle is parked in front. Erin pulls into a spot towards the back of the parking lot. Only a metal barrier stands between her vehicle and the magnificent scenic overlook. She exits her Hyundai Kona, opens the rear driver's side door, and pulls out a tripod. With no one around before daybreak, she removes her tan trench coat to reveal a sleek, green summer dress with no bra underneath. The chill in the mountain air hardens Erin's nipples, much to her delight.

Erin sets up her tripod near the edge of the parking lot, surveying the glorious mountain range behind her. Waiting, she watches a weathered blue Chevy pickup drive past her towards the entrance ramp in the distance. Once the coast is clear, Erin positions the tripod accordingly, places her iPhone on it, then sets it up to record a video. It's a process she has mastered many times over.

At first light, Erin smiles devilishly, knowing full well John Gillies never envisioned his daughter would return to his favorite spot for a moment like this. Erin has become adept at defying her parents' expectations over the years. These days, she hardly thinks twice about her penchant for naughty thrills. She recalls more words of wisdom John imparted to his only child, not long before his death.

Celebrate the ruin, my dear. Life is short and sweet, but also sour. God needs the Devil to keep the universe moving. You can't have one without the other. Yin and yang, good and evil, they're all there. When you look in the mirror, it's all staring back at you. We admire our feats of strength. Don't forget to accept our shortcomings.

On the verge of tears, Erin wipes her eyes and gently nods, bringing herself back to the present. She cautiously looks both ways for potential onlookers, making sure to check the windows of the diner as well. With no one watching, she centers her mind and body and hits the record button. In full performance mode, she walks a few feet in front of her phone and starts her missive.

"Hey, babe! So, this is my absolute favorite spot in the entire world," she begins in a narrative voice. "Right over there is Signal Knob, which is at the peak of Massanutten Mountain. It's quite an awesome sight, isn't it? These gorgeous hills and valleys... Nothing but greenery and blue skies. Well, they will be blue once the sun rises. And speaking of w hich..."

Suddenly, Erin reaches into her cleavage and effortlessly pulls out both of her ample breasts.

"I was thinking maybe you'd like to survey *these* peaks right here," she resumes in a sultrier tone. "I think it's time for *you* to rise and shine as well. There's just enough light. Well, either way, you can't miss these beacons. What is it, you said? I have a body made for sin? So, tell me, would you care to climb these mountains with me? Because I sure as hell would want *you* to explore THIS heavenly view!"

With a cool, calculated glare, Erin peers through the lens of her camera, peaks dangling prominently, wind whipping her hair. With the boldness of a lion, she delivers her closing remarks.

"What do you think... Mister Scott? Did you bring your walking stick? If not, I'm pretty sure I can find one for you!"

Erin lets those last words sink in before snapping out of her secret internet persona. She hastily places her tits back into her dress, retrieves her phone, and packs up her tripod. Shivering from the brisk autumn air, she grabs her trench coat and wraps it around her body once more, just in the nick of time. A grey Ford Taurus turns off the main road and pulls into the parking lot two spots down. She gazes up at the sign for the Strasburg Diner and checks the time on her phone.

Twelve minutes after seven. *Why not?*

Having captured the great outdoors in a most tantalizing fashion, Erin walks up the ramp towards the entrance but stops midway. It dawns on her that she starts her new corporate position tomorrow. For the first time in years, she doesn't have to fly to her next destination. Erin has finally landed and arrived safely. A sense of relief and satisfaction washes over her, for she has conquered yet another mountain. All that's left for Erin to do is log into her fun Instagram account, send her video to its lucky recipient, and celebrate the ruin with the diner's version of a grand slam.

Episode Three: Black Number One

1) Erin: The Absence of Color

Welcome to North Carolina.

Literally, it's a sign on the highway, an uplifting checkpoint for northerners traveling to Florida. For Erin Gillies, it signals something different, the beginning of an endless cavalcade of shameless advertisements and a trigger for fond memories.

The last time John and Karen Gillies took their daughter on vacation was when she was fifteen. Her parents had chosen to drive down to Orlando rather than fly, solely for the experience.

For Erin, it was a trip to remember. Once the Virginia natives crossed into North Carolina, the billboards unceremoniously appeared like rays of sunshine peeking through the clouds. One by one, they seemingly grew larger and more outlandish, promising a huge payoff several miles ahead.

The light at the end of the proverbial tunnel was neither a geodesic sphere nor a fairytale castle. Instead, it was an enigmatic unknown, referred to in a bold, cartoonish font as something called "South of the Border."

Even as her father assured her the payoff was not worth the buildup, young Erin's curiosity grew. Sure enough, when the family of three reached the I-95 state line that separated the Carolinas, the promised utopia gave way to a campy, unfulfilling compound.

Still fascinated, Erin gazed through the backseat window as the overblown, Mexican-themed gift shop on steroids faded into the distance.

Since that day, Erin has harbored a morbid curiosity for moderately sized tourist attractions. As a former flight attendant, she has flown over every border in the contiguous United States and seen every tourist trap known to humankind. Her previous home in central Florida was virtually one huge bastion for visitors, too.

Resting on the outskirts of Orlando's ICON Park is Erin's favorite International Drive hangout, Roberto's. The popular Mexican restaurant is where Erin met Scott Prichard.

Before she'd allowed the alcohol to fuel her desires, he was simply a mild-mannered twenty-eight-year-old realtor who'd recently started working for his father's brokerage. After consuming four apple martinis, her inebriated state had convinced her he was a smooth-talking, sex god who needed to have his body ravaged by a real woman with real curves.

They'd both established each other's situations. Erin was happily single and frequently on the move, sometimes with little to no notice. Scott was in between relationships and just needed a little pussy to pet, a lot of tits to marvel at, and a good lay in the meantime. Erin warmly obliged him, and they agreed to some fun with no strings attached.

Erin and Scott never exchanged phone numbers, but with a plethora of social media options available to them, there'd been no need to do so. In fact, Scott was happy to partake in Erin's side hustle and purchase the sultry videos she produced through her Instagram account, 'RedheadBombs407,' for the usual sum of fifty bucks.

Before long, he claimed to have found love, yet he remained one of her many frequent customers. Out of respect for his relationship, she did not offer to see him again, instead keeping the conversation scarce and friendly, yet occasionally spicy.

To Erin, the ends justified the means. If Scott had a moral dilemma, that was not her concern.

To Erin's surprise, on the day she began her new job, Scott had unexpectedly messaged her, asking if she was available to meet once more. Though she was committed to her new life in Virginia, Erin responded in the affirmative, advising him she was driving down to her old haunts one last time the following weekend to pick up the last of her personal belongings.

And so, on this sunny yet chilly December Saturday, almost thirty years after her family's initial trip to the "Sunshine State," Erin is behind the wheel enroute to her apartment in Orlando. She has not traveled this road by car since the day John Gillies disregarded the billboards and stayed the course.

Like her father, she too is set on reaching her destination, one final encounter with the captivating young man who grabbed her attention some nine months prior.

However, despite her desire to offer Scott his going away present, Erin needs to cross an item off her bucket list, simply for personal edification. Those same eerily bombastic highway road signs cry for her attention, refusing to be ignored. Before she goes downtown on Scott, the auburn bombshell must go "South of the Border."

The crass sombrero tower fades in from the distance as Erin draws closer to exit 1B. Still intrigued after all these years, but ready for the foretold disappointment, she pulls off I-95 towards Route 301 and 501 North. Once she makes the left at the end of the ramp and proceeds over the state line, the lurid landmarks that surround her leave no doubt that Erin is no longer in North Carolina.

Multiple large and creepy statues representing Diego the mascot, a thinly veiled caricature of Mexican stereotypes, loom on both sides of the road. His smiling visage is meant to attract patrons. The official welcome sign promises hot tamales, nachos, and chili dogs.

Further ahead is a long one-story building that sells fireworks. Erin cringes at the idea of purchasing them, instead turning into the parking lot for Diego's Border Shop. Like all other signs on this road, the arch in front of the building is loud and imposing.

Uncharacteristically dressed in a casual grey sweater and blue jeans, Erin scurries through the massive space and into the shop's restroom at the rear of the store. Moments later, she returns and saunters through the endless cavalcade of t-shirts, magnets, pens, keychains, and other miscellaneous items branded with the tourist trap's custom logo. Their offerings are plentiful but standard.

All she needs is a souvenir trinket to mark her one and only appearance in this grand fiesta town. A display of Mexican scarves next to the register intrigues Erin. As she stops to stare at the numerous Aztec designs, a shop employee abruptly approaches her from behind.

"I turned some warm blankets into comfy scarves," the lady advises.

Startled, Erin spins around and finds a smiling, heavy-set, middle-aged woman, outwardly proud of her craftiness.

"Oh, wow!" Erin exclaims as she taps her chest. "Yes. Yes, they look wonderful."

"They're made from authentic Mexican serape," the lady continues. "Each one is seventy-two inches long and nine inches wide. You can drape it across your shoulders, tie it around your neck, maybe hold it in place with a simple knot."

With the mention of nine inches, Erin's mind automatically defaults to the gutter, to thoughts of the activities that await her and

Scott this evening and a particular appendage she can't wait to touch. She tries in vain not to chuckle at the salesperson's innocent comment.

"They're beautiful," Erin remarks, approaching the display with its various color schemes. One in particular draws her interest, a black woven pattern with white trim. Erin reaches out to feel the material, wanting eyes negating her poker face.

"That's a good one," says the salesperson. "The others are so bright and sunny. I wanted to create one for the pitch-black night."

A peculiar urge overcomes Erin. Typically drawn to primary colors, something inside of her feels a pull towards the absence of color. Unable to resist, Erin declares her intentions. "I'll take this one."

"Great, let's ring you up."

Erin returns to her vehicle, paper shopping bag in hand, scarf inside of it. With the push of a button, she starts her Hyundai Kona remotely. Just as Erin shuts the car door to resume her journey, she receives a message on her alternate Instagram account. She peers at her phone and melts at both the sender and the content.

Gazing back at her screen, Erin sees not the name of the man she is planning to meet, but instead the name of a man with whom she has recently developed a steamy casual relationship. With an earnest smile, she mutters softly and deeply, "Bryce."

> Wish you were here, Miss Erin. I know you're tying up loose ends in Florida this weekend, but I still can't get your massive tits out of my head. I know you're thinking about me too. Let's do something when you get back.

Erin hurriedly and excitedly taps the screen to respond accordingly. Just as quickly, she opts to go into her camera app instead. She gently rubs her eyes with a tissue, fixes her fiery, bunned red hair, licks her lips, and hits the record button from the comfort of her driver's seat.

"Hey, Mister Bryce!" she begins using her sultry, inviting deep voice. "Looks like you blinked first, which means you get to go south of the border on me first the next time we meet."

Erin briefly pauses to chuckle at her own joke, then continues.

"Wouldn't you know it, that's exactly where I am right now. Just stopping in for a little lunch here in South Carolina. Maybe I'll stretch my legs and walk around the gift shop. I think you know how well I can stretch my legs. Perhaps I can help you stretch *yours*. Mmmm?"

Erin's smile widens as her tongue playfully massages her lips from left to right. Allowing a moment to let that sexy image sink in, she then resumes her speech.

"Don't worry about the PayPal, Mister Bryce. Consider this a free one. I'm not exactly dressed for the occasion. Besides, you've got plenty of content to keep you occupied until I come back... And, cum, we will!"

With her typical raised eyebrows, Erin delivers her final salvo in a cool whisper.

"I still feel your hot seed inside me, Mister Bryce. The question is, how *long* can you wait to have me again?"

Grinning devilishly, Erin stops the video and promptly sends it to Bryce, figuring he will pleasure himself to her message long before they meet again. As she places her hand on the gear shift, she realizes there is one more man who may want a similar update.

Reaching for her phone, Erin clicks on Instagram. She opens her direct messages, expecting to find 'ScottPrich203' third or fourth from the top, as he always is. Instead, a perplexed Erin sees no such name on her list. Undeterred, she clicks on the hourglass icon to search for him.

No such handle exists.

Did you change your username? Erin wonders. She searches for his actual name: Scott Prichard. Several users with the same name appear, but much to her chagrin, not the one she knows.

Instinctively, Erin switches to Facebook. Even though she and Scott were not friends on the app, she had stalked his profile a few times in the past. Each time, his profile had insisted he was in a relationship. Regardless, the Scott Prichard she knows has disappeared from the metaverse.

Erin slumps over in her seat, trying to put two and two together. It's not exactly the first time she's been ghosted, but somehow, this hurts deeply. Inexplicably, she feels a sense of loss.

Erin pulls away from the souvenir shop and continues further south towards her final destination. Her heart aches from the blatant disrespect. She has four hundred and ninety miles left to ponder exactly where it all went wrong.

2) Bryce: Operant Conditioning

Storm clouds roll into Northern Virginia as Bryce Palmieri sits uncomfortably on a black leather sofa in his living room. Though physically refreshed after his brief nap, his mind is still drained, still scattered. Several times, he's tried to string his thoughts together into coherent sentences in an email to his boss, Mitch, to no avail.

Irritated by his inability to do so, he slams his laptop closed and decides to relax.

Biding his time before his lunch companion arrives, Bryce turns on The Weather Channel and sinks into the sofa. Dressed in his navy-blue Richmond Spiders t-shirt and grey sweatpants, he watches intently as the national forecast shifts to the southeastern part of the country.

Bryce perks up, unconsciously smiling as he discovers nothing but bright, blue skies in the immediate future for the "Sunshine State." His mind flashing to Erin, he briefly considers checking in on her but decides to leave well enough alone. After all, it had taken considerable restraint to suppress his arousal while still in the comfort of his first-class seat when he'd received her earlier video message.

Before long, his lingering thoughts are interrupted by the simultaneous sound of thunder and knocking. At first, Bryce hesitates, unsure whether the noise came from his front door or if a neighboring condo resident had slammed theirs. After a moment, Bryce rises, walks over to the bay window overlooking the building's front parking lot, and confirms his guest has indeed arrived at five minutes to one.

Bryce opens the door to a towering, broad-shouldered presence – a five-foot-ten goddess of a woman. Adorned in all black from head to toe, from her sequined leather jacket, tank top, and jeans to her St. John's Bay Rayford boots, she grins fiendishly at the sight of him. Her thick yet toned physique makes Bryce gasp under his breath. Long, curled, black hair overshadows her piercing brown eyes.

"Heather," he greets her. "You're early."

Furrowing her brow, she tilts her head and unleashes a soft chuckle. "You make it sound like that's a bad thing," she states. "You're not busy with *her*, are you?"

"No," Bryce quickly confirms. "She's down in Florida."

Stepping aside, he lets Heather enter. Despite his best attempts to remain stoic, her slow, self-assured strut disarms him.

"Going somewhere?" she wonders as she glances across the room at his blue carry-on.

"Just came from somewhere," Bryce clarifies. "We're opening up a new restaurant in Canonsburg, about twenty miles south of Pittsburgh."

"Ah, ever the world traveler," remarks Heather as she turns to face him. "Sorry about last weekend, by the way."

"No sweat," replies Bryce. "How's the little guy?"

"Oh, he's fine now," she answers with a hint of indifference. "Yeah, they made it halfway down to see his dad, pulled into a rest stop, and then Mikey started throwing up."

"Aw, man. That sucks," he sympathizes.

Slowly, Heather removes her leather jacket and drapes it gently over the arm of Bryce's sofa. As she does, her tank top hugs her chest perfectly, accentuating her 44DDs. Bryce can't help but stare at her sturdy, bare arms. She grins when she catches him.

"You dyed your hair," he notices. "It looks nice."

"Thanks."

"All blacked out and no place to go," Bryce jokes.

"I needed a change," she says, matter-of-factly. "I was a dirty blonde for ten years, pretty much since the day I met Zach. Change is good."

"Yep."

Without another word, Heather saunters down the hall towards the bedroom. Bryce follows, keeping a safe distance between them, awestruck by her stunningly dark new appearance.

"Do you want to eat first or, uh, play first?" he slyly asks.

Heather slips into Bryce's bedroom without answering. Unable to see her, Bryce hesitates, waiting outside for her response. For a moment, she's silent. After a couple of seconds, she reacts.

"Well, this is new. Hey, Bryce, check this out."

Curious, he enters his bedroom. As he steps through the doorway, the jet-black vixen is nowhere to be seen. Just out of sight, she lies in wait for him by his sliding closet door.

"Heath—"

As fast as the lightning strikes in the distance, she lunges at Bryce, spearing him against the opposite wall. He grunts in pain, but just as quickly as she'd sprung, Heather places her hands on his cheekbones and delivers a powerful kiss.

Stunned by her sudden attack and stimulated by Heather's skilled tongue, Bryce wraps his arms around her back. She playfully massages his earlobes and the sides of his short blonde hair. All the while, her tongue slides down Bryce's neck, eliciting soft exhales.

With his member rising considerably, he attempts to walk her backwards to the bed, only to be cut off by Heather's hand suddenly clamping down on his balls. Bryce grunts and falls back against the wall.

He and Heather have played these rough-and-tumble games many times over. Always craving a sex life full of unusual foreplay and roleplay, Heather had dumped his former college baseball teammate, Bobby Downing, some twenty-five years earlier.

With Bryce, she'd found a willing participant. While Heather's current spouse prefers the standard bedroom fare, she still desires more, which is why she still insists on seeing Bryce after all these years. Perpetually single with a libido stronger than ever, he gladly withstands her aggressively fondling his genitalia, for the endgame is always satisfying.

"Ohhh, Heather!" he cries out in a mixture of pleasure and pain.

"Now that I have your attention, let's talk, big boy," she demands with an icy stare.

Trapped in limbo, Bryce begs the powerful woman in black to release her iron grip. "Ah! Please, Heather!"

"Oh, I'll please you," she declares. "Just as soon as we get something perfectly clear."

Heather lets go of his groin, immediately prompting a sigh of relief.

"I know we've done this a million times before," he reasons while doubled over. "But can't you give me advanced notice before you do that?"

"Well, that wouldn't be as fun, now, would it?" she coldly retorts, gently tugging on a fistful of his shirt. Guiding Bryce away from the wall, she backs against the foot of his bed.

"I want you to tell me a story," Heather demands with a soft voice. "A boy toy story. Because you *are* my boy toy."

Sensing where the conversation is going, Bryce diplomatically attempts to resolve the issue with his notoriously possessive counterpart.

"Before we get too carried away, let's remember the rules," he explains. "We come and go as we please. You do you and I do me, and when the opportunity presents itself, we do each other. Besides, you already have someone else."

Rain begins to fall outside, providing a foreboding soundtrack. Softening her stance, Heather reaches underneath Bryce's shirt and calmly strokes his pecs. Smiling and nodding, she arches her back, accentuating her ample breasts.

"You make a strong argument," she admits.

Unable to resist Heather's feminine wiles, Bryce casually stares down the length of her cleavage, then peers back up at her. He grins mightily, believing he has made his point and that they're in for the usual rough yet pleasureful bedroom fun.

Deliberately, Heather lowers her body, lifting the bottom of Bryce's t-shirt. He casually raises his arms, allowing her to remove his shirt entirely. Serenely, she runs her hands up and down the length of his shoulder blades, then moves behind him, sweetly rubbing his left nipple.

Bryce becomes further entranced by the sound of Heather's heavy breath in his ears. Seizing the opportunity to finally disrobe, she delightfully spins him around so that he can watch her remove her tank top. With uncanny precision, Heather unclasps her bra and frees her ample tits, drawing a wide grin from Bryce. Ready to begin, he squats down to unzip and remove her boots.

"I won't make you kiss them just yet," Heather remarks as she giggles.

"I think it's your turn to kiss mine," he says as he rises up to unbuckle her belt. "You promised."

"We'll see about that," she muses as she drops her jeans and kicks them off. With no wasted time or movement, she reaches for Bryce's sweatpants. Carefully, she pulls them down over his noticeable erection, and teases going down on him. Instead, she rises up again, building suspense and furthering his urges.

Motioning towards the bed, Heather leads Bryce around the side and kisses him passionately before gently collapsing with him onto the mattress.

Heather scoots up towards the headboard and positions herself behind Bryce. With them both seated, she runs her fingernails down the length of his spine. The sensation causes Bryce to arch his body. Suddenly, she finds her opening, quickly pinning his left arm behind his back and wrapping her right arm around his neck.

"Gotcha, big boy!" Heather declares before cackling.

Knowing her grip isn't tight enough to cut off his air supply, Bryce laughs along with her.

"Yup, you won this round."

"As I was saying, you make a strong argument, but not strong enough!" Heather states with a wily glare.

Ensnaring him even more, she wraps her legs around his waist. Bryce beams at her, trapped by the Amazonian woman's scissor hold. It's just tight enough to render him incapable of moving, but not enough to hurt. The thrill of being trapped by the strong, sexy vixen makes Bryce feel alive and hard.

"Well, looks who's *up* to the task," a joyful Heather responds. "It's unfortunate and ironic because you let me down, boy toy. You went and pursued that redheaded jezebel after I reminded you she only wants you for cheap thrills."

"Ah. The point emerges," he grunts through short, labored breaths. "Cheap thrills, huh? What do you call this?"

"I call it operant conditioning," Heather playfully retorts. "We've talked about this."

"She's here now," Bryce advises.

"Oh, *is* she here? She's not in Florida?"

"She is. She's... coming back."

Heather smirks at Bryce's statement. Like a boa constrictor incapacitating its helpless prey, her grip intensifies, eliciting loud moans.

"Ooh, this is my favorite part, big Bryce," she reminds him. "Pushing you just a *little* bit more, testing your limits, and then... Ohhhhh!"

Her right arm finally loosens, gliding down the length of his chest, still keeping his arm pinned to his side. Heather deviously flicks Bryce's nipple, then feverishly massages it, prompting the air in Bryce's chest to escape in spurts.

"Ahhhh!" he firmly exclaims.

"Ah, yes. Tell me. Who was there for you when she ghosted you last summer, huh?" she inquires. "Who's been here for you all these years?"

Aware of her mind games, Bryce struggles to emote his objections with her last statement.

"You use me for your sick fantasies," he responds meekly.

"Don't get all sanctimonious on me now," she remarks. "We use each other. It's been that way from day one and you know it. I understand she's got your head all twisted, but I'll always be here for you."

Calmly stroking Bryce's chest and kissing the back of his neck, Heather puts him at ease for the moment. His dick quickly hardens to its full, impressive eight inches.

"Oh, Heather. We should have stayed together."

She laughs heartily at his thesis. "Oh, big Bryce, we've been over that time and time again," she coolly replies. "You were always on the road making the big bucks while Zach was home making babies and being the perfect father... something you know you could never be."

Bryce has no answer, but Heather doesn't let her statement resonate. She knows he hasn't seen Erin since the morning after their first meeting. His urges rise with every passing day, so she's well aware that she can get her kicks in while catering to Bryce's needs.

"But there is something you can be," she reminds him. "Something you have always been. You'll always be my *favorite* boy toy, with your stunning physique, your glowing blonde hair, and your glorious six-pack. Oh my God, Bryce. You look even better than those magnificent, muscular cover models. How I want you…"

Though she has lessened her grip on Bryce, he presses against her immaculate figure enthusiastically. Even in times like these, the blonde stud harkens back to his longing to be held and nurtured, something he had very little of in his youth. Her deep, dense warmth seeps through every inch of his skin. Heather allows this, stroking his ego as well as his body, increasing his desire for sweet release.

"Yes, Heather. I want you!"

"I knew you did," she asserts with evil intent. "Deep down, way down in the *cockles* of your heart, you need a woman like *me*."

Heather lets go of Bryce, only to shift her body on top of him. She flips her mane in a dramatic fashion, grinning mightily. Instantaneous pleasure overwhelms Bryce as Heather deftly guides his cock inside her pussy.

Smiling wickedly, she raises her arms and corrals her hair, writhing in a rhythm that falls perfectly in synch with him. Her remarkably strong yet feminine guns entice him. Her swaying tits further hypnotize Bryce, whose eyes follow along with every bounce.

"Oh… wow!" he decrees.

"Oh, Bryce. Who's your big momma?" she inquires.

"You are! Oh, Big Momma!" he cries out as he arches his head and neck backwards, perilously close to firing a week's worth of ammo already.

Not even close to her own orgasm, Heather responds if only to encourage her boy toy over the hump.

"I was so wet for you the last time," she informs him, panting sensually. "I almost pulled over on my way back home. Just thinking about you makes me cum! Oh, big Bryce! I'm gonna *cum*!"

Heather's deliberately chosen last word lingers just long enough for Bryce to reach the summit. He trembles violently and shakes as he explodes with incredible intensity. The force of his burst even surprises Heather, who is now even more aroused.

"Ohh! Holy shit, Bryce!" she bellows, attempting to sneak in a few more post-ejaculation thrusts for her own satisfaction.

Having freed his heavy load, Bryce lays back trying to recalibrate his breathing. His mind racing once again, he barely notices Heather disembarking to finger herself. Moaning vociferously, her face mirrors Bryce's earlier expression as she looks back at him and achieves her own orgasm.

After a few seconds of cooling down, Heather references a separate discussion from years prior.

"You don't even think about going in bareback anymore," she humorously remarks. "I remember when I first had the procedure done. You were so nervous. The first thing you asked me was, 'Are you sure you can't get pregnant?'"

As Heather cackles away, Bryce tries to remain indifferent but fails and sighs indignantly. "It was a valid concern of mine. You know I couldn't take on that kind of responsibility at the time. Just like you said, I wasn't dad material."

"Jesus, it was a joke," she retorts, dismissively rolling her eyes.

Slowly, they both rise up, find their respective discarded articles of clothing, and get dressed. When Heather turns to Bryce, his eyes, no longer clouded by lust, reveal an equal amount of fulfillment and contemplation.

As he gazes out the bedroom window at a grey, wet parking lot, he wonders to himself, *Who do I want more, the woman who's taken but chooses me or the woman who isn't but chooses her freedom?*

Heather senses Bryce is having second thoughts and attempts to distract him and garner sympathy by apologizing for hurting his feelings. Heather holds her breath long enough to redden her face. Appearing to be on the verge of tears, she firmly hugs him and places her head against his chest.

"I'm sorry!" she cries out. "I just don't want to see you get hurt again!"

Bryce holds her gently out of obligation. Even though he questions her sincerity, he doesn't wish to argue. Gingerly, he pulls away and rubs her upper arms.

"I appreciate your concern," he notes. "Really, I do, but I'm a big boy, like you astutely pointed out."

Heather smirks and looks back at him perplexed. "Astutely? You been reading the dictionary?" she asks while chuckling.

"Just trying to broaden my horizons."

Heather disregards his declaration. "Remember what I said. I know you, Bryce. I know you keep things bottled up. You reach for that pie in the sky, as opposed to the pie right in front of you."

Bryce's genuine grin dissolves into a look of confusion as Heather abruptly walks into the bedroom to put on her jacket.

"No late lunch, I guess?" he wonders as he follows her.

"I'm afraid not," she says. "Zach and Mikey should be done with laser bounce soon, or laser tag, or whatever it's called."

Bryce's eyes pierce Heather's like daggers. He seizes an opportunity to deliver a carefully crafted retort to Heather's earlier statement.

"Ah. So, the pie isn't really mine, is it? I only get sloppy seconds."

Heather grins, appreciating Bryce's wit and the validity of his comment. She starts to leave, then turns to offer a counterpoint out of sheer jealousy.

"She's probably having one last quickie with her old boyfriend. You know how that goes. I'll bet you dollars to donuts you're not her first priority, either."

"Hey, I've always been my first priority," he shoots back. "Like I said, we do what we do when we want, how we want. Besides, I didn't have to let you come over here."

The woman in black stands up straight to give Bryce a sexy lasting image before responding. Deliberately, she looks at his groin, a sharp reminder of which head Bryce ultimately chooses to listen to.

"Oh, yes you did. You sure as hell did."

The spent regional sales manager does not move an inch when Heather strolls through his living room and exits the condo. As the thunderstorm fades into the distance, Bryce's newfound resolve disappears. *Where had it all gone wrong?*

3) Erin: Miss Black

Saturday night's twilight has fallen on International Drive. Beneath a darkening sky, a despondent Erin, wearing a black Harper Clip Chiffon short-sleeve pullover, sits and waits for her best friend, Stephanie Pronger, in the outdoor seating area of Roberto's.

She has procured the last of her belongings. Now, they reside in the back seat of her car, parked across the street at the Icon Hotel, where she will attempt to sleep for the night before starting her journey home.

While she waits, Erin tries to count the number of times she's been used over the years by young men who only see her as a wondrous object. The fact that Scott had specifically asked for this visit, only to vanish, echoes a more painful memory.

Shortly after her high school graduation, John Gillies, weakened by cancer but strong in his convictions, had promised Erin he'd be waiting for her when she returned from her hiking trip. Yet, when she arrived back home in Fredericksburg, he was comatose. Her father was gone forever the very next day. He and his daughter never said their proper goodbyes.

Though vastly different circumstances, Erin equates Scott's failure to keep his word with John's body failing him before she could see him alive one last time. Here today, gone tomorrow. It's a common refrain in Erin's life, though none of her previous one-night stands knew better than to make grandiose promises they couldn't keep.

It shouldn't be like this. Stephanie has advised Erin on numerous occasions that men stop playing games after the age of forty. After all, she and her boyfriend, Terry, have been dating for six months. Both are recently divorced and free from the perils of youthful ignorance. The two of them had partied in their twenties, enjoyed multiple partners, then wound up marrying the wrong person.

For Stephanie and Terry, their thirties were an emotional roller coaster, leading them to grow apart from their respective former spouses.

Now comes the happy ending, according to Stephanie. She claims the early forties are the best time for lovers. After all, you're still young enough to explore sensual pleasures and finally old enough to do it right. "It's never too late."

Erin has heard the words many times over and processed them. However, platitudes do not erase actions, nor do they undo misfortunes. They cannot bring back her father. They do not grant the approval of her mother, still back home in Virginia. They won't give Erin back the six years she wasted on Adam, nor will they return the fourteen years she has spent flying all over the country trying to forget hi m.

Erin's former therapist had rightfully surmised she may be running from her problems instead of coming to terms with them and moving forward.

Of course, that path came with its own problems. Words do not cancel out the numerous encounters Erin endured with Swan Airlines passengers who only wanted to join the Mile High Club. In the past two years, she all but gave up trying to earn the travelers' respect. She'd decided that if God gave her a body made for sin, she may as well take full advantage of it.

Stephanie is the only woman who knows of Erin's secret side hustle, the only one Erin trusts. Naturally, her friend has expressed concern that the now-former flight attendant will somehow be outed. Erin refuses to listen, maintaining that she is simply living her "best life."

Safely nestled under an umbrella, the forty-four-year-old gazes out towards the iconic four-hundred-foot-tall observation wheel, clearly visible within a quarter-mile radius. Regularly, families with young children flock towards the booming landmark. Its enclosed, air-conditioned glass capsules offer sweeping views of the Orlando skyline.

The experience of riding in the wheel had once thrilled her. Not anymore. Erin has literally been there, done that, and bought the t-shirt.

A busboy named Juan walks over to pour water into both empty glasses, to which Erin softly replies, "Thank you." While he works, she pretends to look at the menu placed neatly in front of her, but her mind is not on food either. Tonight, no water, no alcohol, and no medication can curb her lack of enthusiasm.

Moments later, adorned with her custom blackout shades and palm tree charm necklace, Stephanie bursts into the outdoor seating area, arms wide open to greet her friend. "Girl!" she yells as Erin rises from her seat to hug her. "My dad was late arriving, and Matthew was acting up," Stephanie explains.

"No worries," Erin replies with less than her usual fire. "God forbid his mommy go out for a dinner with adults."

Stephanie laughs and swiftly plants herself in the chair next to Erin, her back to the walkway. She whips off her sunglasses and places them atop her brown mane. Her eyes stare a hole through the preoccupied redhead as she leans in for a heart-to-heart.

"What's wrong?" Stephanie asks assertively. "I know you. Don't lie to me."

Erin looks down and massages the outside of her full water glass. Condensation wets her fingers as she takes a long, hard breath before speaking.

"Oh, I'm just having another panic attack."

"What's wrong?" Her friend sternly repeats.

Erin lifts her head, eyes filled with tears, and reveals her deep-rooted issue. "Everyone leaves me, Steph. My father, my mother, Dean— everyone I've ever gotten close to, and I just can't figure out why even Scott ghosted me."

"Scott?" Steph replies. "You mean that little shit who was all into you for, like, a week and then found someone else?"

"Yeah, I know," says Erin. "It's just that he asked to see me this weekend, and now he's suddenly disappeared. I don't get it."

Stephanie waves her hand as if to tell her bestie to wipe the slate clean. "Not worth it. His loss. Move on. I mean, you and I both know it was just going to be one last fuck for good measure. You can get that from anybody."

"I know, but that's not the point," Erin answers. "It's the rejection. The lack of respect. The lack of closure."

"Oh, honey. You gotta focus on what you have, not what you don't have," Stephanie points out. "Besides, didn't you have that date with Brian from eHarmony a couple of weeks ago?"

Erin grins cheekily and sways in her chair. "Weeellll, not exactly."

"What do you mean not exactly?" wonders a dumbfounded Stephanie.

A spark gleams in Erin's eyes for the first time since she arrived in the magic city. "You'll never guess who showed up that night," she answers.

"Who?"

"You remember the guy I told you about?" a beaming Erin asks. "The one I knew from high school who flew down to visit me last summer?"

About to take a drink, Stephanie slams down her glass. "No way! Bryce?"

"Yup!"

"Whoa!" Stephanie is clearly elated. "Did he know you were going to be there?"

A gust of wind whips Erin's hair, covering her face. "He said he didn't. I'm not sure if I believe him. I mean, it seems too coincidental."

Stephanie furrows her brow and smiles. "So, he showed up during your date?"

"The date never happened," Erin acknowledges. "Brian was late. Bryce showed up a couple of minutes after six. We locked eyes and it was all over. It was like we were the only two people in the room."

"Oooh, like in one of those rom-coms," Stephanie says. "They go through this whole rigmarole, they finally get together at the end and live happily ever after." Erin's bestie then raises her eyebrows suggestively. "And then they fuck each other's brains out," she bellows.

"First of all, I am *not* rom-com material, girlfriend," retorts Erin. "You've seen my Insta. You know what I'm all about. No, Bryce and I are only interested in casual sex."

"You're lying to me," Stephanie immediately deadpans. "I saw that look in your eyes when I said his name. You're smitten."

"I'm *so* not smitten. I assure you." Erin pauses and her lips form a wide smile. "But we did fuck each other's brains out, and it was *amazing!*"

A delighted Stephanie gasps and pantomimes fanning herself with her free hand. "Yeah, bitch!"

Abruptly, a middle-aged man with slicked jet-black hair wearing a white shirt and black pants approaches.

"Hi, ladies. Did anyone take your order yet?" he asks.

"Nope," the ladies reply in unison.

Gently, he bows his head. "I apologize. I'll send Kristen right over. Can I you get some drinks in the meantime?"

Erin pauses for a split second, then lifts her head. "Landshark?"

Stephanie chimes in, "Same."

"Coming right up."

Erin thanks him. Stephanie takes a long sip of her water, then bulges her eyes.

"Mmmm," she grunts while slamming her glass down and wiping her mouth.

"You didn't tell Bryce you chickened out that day, did you?"

"No, I didn't," Erin confirms. "He still thinks I had to catch that last-minute flight out of town. I just... I panicked, you know? He was one of those guys. I was sending him the videos. I hadn't seen him in what, twenty-five years? I was scared, to be honest."

"You had no problem going home with him last weekend, right?" Stephanie reasons. "Was it his place or your place?"

"His. And yeah, I just went with my gut, and now that we've met in person and had real conversations, I'm perfectly fine being around him."

"Obviously," Stephanie jokes.

"Ha, yeah," says Erin. "But last summer, I just wasn't sure. I was still a flight attendant. I had so much going on, you know."

The forty-two-year-old Icon Hotel manager reaches across the table and places her warm fingers on Erin's left hand.

"Catch flights, not feelings," she rationalizes.

"Exactly!" Erin answers with conviction. "I mean, I can't catch feelings if I'm not there to catch them. Right?"

Juan the busboy returns with the requisite chips and salsa. Halfway through swallowing her first chip, Erin can no longer contain the truth of what her mind and body want.

"God, I need a good fuck right now. I can't believe Scott bailed on me. We had plans. I wish Bryce was here. I'm going to see him when I get back, but..."

She looks both ways, then behind her, surveying the situation at the bar inside the restaurant. Erin leans in and catches Stephanie's full attention before revealing her impromptu idea.

"You know what? I'm getting laid anyway. Some guy's getting lucky tonight."

The two ladies share a genuine, hearty laugh as Kristen approaches to take their respective orders. After they both request fish tacos, Erin looks up towards the big wheel, which is now illuminated in purple against the dusk. A thrilled Stephanie encourages her friend to follow through.

"Look at you, Tits McGee," she humorously remarks. "A few minutes ago, you were ready to take the Pepsi Plunge off the top of that wheel. Now, you're talking about getting railed. What are you gonna do in Virginia without me?"

"Get railed," Erin replies without hesitation. "Good and hard."

A young lady passerby in a butterfly-printed hoodie catches Erin's attention. The woman's long black hair blows in the wind as she proceeds down the walking path away from view.

"I wonder how I'd look in black," Erin ponders.

"No, no! Don't mess with success, hun," replies Stephanie. "You've got natural red hair. People would kill for that."

"Yeah, but I've had natural red hair for, like, four decades. I also have naturally huge tits, as you so dutifully pointed out."

Erin points at her chest to further illustrate her point. "I could have green or purple hair, but *these* are my calling card, baby! They walk in ten minutes before I do."

"Shit, yeah!"

The rest of the meal between the two best friends proceeds nicely. Their espresso martinis and apple strudels go down even better. Shortly after seven, Stephanie readies herself to leave, insisting on paying as a going-away present.

"Thanks, babe!" Erin says.

"No problem," replies Stephanie. "So, what are you thinking tonight? Young lion or silver fox?"

"I think I'll just go across the street to the Rusted Roof," states Erin. "Believe me, it won't take long to find someone. It never does."

"I don't need to tell you to be careful," answers Stephanie. "Oops, I just did."

With a shrug and a giggle, Stephanie and Erin hug and part ways. Erin throws her travel purse over her neck and shoulder, then walks inside the restaurant to use the restroom.

As she's about to leave Roberto's, she catches a glimpse of three young men eyeing her from the corner of the bar. When she glances their way, they quickly retreat and pretend to focus their attentions elsewhere.

This is standard fare for the bombshell, always the belle of the ball. A deliciously naughty smile forms on Erin's face. It's clear she doesn't need to pretend to be just another punk rocker at the Rusted Roof. One of those three men is bound to be unattached, and even if none of them were, that's never stopped her from convincing a taken, sex-deprived man to ignore his commitments.

Erin turns on her *charm*, which as she noted earlier, arrives in the room ten minutes before the rest of her. She saunters deliberately towards the trio, each of whom tries desperately not to draw her attention, all unsuccessful at playing it cool.

A tall, lanky blonde takes a step backwards. The man in the middle, a dark-haired bearded prospect follows suit. A noticeable space appears between the two of them and their third man, a beaming brown-haired, polo-shirt-wearing deer in headlights.

Erin locks in on her target. She reaches the bar and turns towards the excited young man to her right. The game is over before a single word is uttered.

"Hello boys!" she says in her sultry voice. "What are we drinking tonight?"

Captivated and speechless, the two young men to her left hesitate to respond. Their friend, however, finds the fortitude to answer.

"Coors Light. How about you?"

"You know, I love a good espresso martini," replies Erin, feigning innocence.

Without hesitation, the man in the polo shirt raises his hand to signal the bartender, who turns around and walks over towards Erin and her unlikely suitor.

"Espresso martini for the lady."

"Why, thank you," Erin says. "And to whom do I owe the pleasure?"

"Huh?"

"Your name, dude," the tall blonde chides.

"Oh! I'm Quinn," he gleefully responds while rolling his eyes at himself and extending his arm. "And you are?"

Erin barely stifles her laughter and gingerly shakes Quinn's hand. "I'm Erin. Nice to meet you."

"Erin, the pleasure is all mine," he responds. Quinn carefully contemplates his next words and promptly stammers over them.

"Well, um. It's not every day I, uh, get to buy a drink for, uh... beautiful lady like yourself."

"Well, Quinn, that's very nice of you," she answers while chuckling. "So, what are you fine gentlemen doing here this evening?"

Pausing to wait for his friends to answer, Quinn realizes they are silently in awe of Erin and equally amazed at her interest in him.

"Watching the Big 12 Championship Game," he responds.

"Oh. Who are we rooting for?" Erin wonders.

"Uh, nobody really," says Quinn. "Just watching it. We go to UCF, and they're not in it this year."

Erin glances over at Quinn's friends who are whispering to each other in confidence. Before she can inquire about their conversation, the bearded man catches wind of her stare and speaks.

"Hey, man. We're gonna jet," he announces with a not-so-subtle nod towards Quinn, indicating they are leaving him to close the deal on his own.

"Alright, cool," Quinn replies. With a couple of manly nods and congratulatory handshakes, his friends leave two twenty-dollar bills on the bar and exit the restaurant. Briefly, Erin turns to watch his wingmen leave. Before she can resume sweet-talking the unwitting Quinn, he breaks the short silence with a most clichéd inquiry.

"So, where are you from?"

"Oh, I'm from here," she answers. "Well, I used to be. I'm actually staying across the street tonight, then returning home to Virginia. Speaking of home, I hope you didn't just lose your ride?"

"Nope," he confirms. "I brought my own car. I'm... I'm good."

Thinking he is successfully wooing Erin, Quinn's smile looms large. He follows up with another vastly predictable question.

"Are you, uh... *with* anyone across the street?"

Deciding she has had enough mundane small talk, Erin switches gears and cuts right to the chase.

"I'm with you," she declares. "Or at least, I will be. It looks like this is becoming a blowout. So, what do you think? Would you like to see another... blowout?"

Quinn marvels silently at her response. Erin reaches into her travel purse and pulls out her spare room key, waving it in front of him. Like a light switch, she abruptly shifts her demeanor from casual to self-assured, the woman who knows she is suave and irresistible.

Unceremoniously, Erin places the card down on the bar and ushers it over to Quinn. His brown eyes bulge almost in perfect synch with the grating sound of the plastic sliding towards him.

"If you'd like to join me for overtime, come to the Icon Hotel. Room 316. It starts in twenty minutes," she offers in her sexy voice.

Before the elated young man can answer, Erin arches her back, knowing his eyes will drift down towards her chest. Beaming back at him, she stands, raises her eyebrow, and places her hand strategically on his upper thigh. Quinn tries unsuccessfully to stifle a soft gasp and closes his eyes. His attempt to hide his public erection becomes futile as Erin gets off her bar stool and leans in towards him.

After glancing over her shoulder to make sure no one's watching, she slyly reaches in between his legs and runs the tips of her fingers over the burgeoning lump beneath his zipper.

"Ohhhh!" a stunned Quinn moans aloud.

"When you can stand up again," whispers Erin. "Come on over. I'll be waiting."

Having easily captured another man's imagination, Erin struts out of Roberto's.

Quinn's eyes remain fixed as he watches her every step of the way until she passes through the open entryway and turns the corner. The lasting image of Erin's curvaceous ass gives him even more reason to follow, but not as quickly as he'd like.

It takes Quinn a solid minute of watching television to distract him long enough to let his cock soften once again. When it does, he places forty dollars cash on the bar and leaves.

Abandoning his car, safely nestled in a nearby parking garage, he turns left, full of desire, and walks across the street to the hotel.

A litany of fleeting thoughts run through Quinn's head as he approaches the entrance.

This is crazy, he surmises. *I can't believe I'm doing this.* For a moment he pauses, letting his mind run wild. *She's amazing - What am I doing?*

A final notion claims him: *This is going to be awesome.*

Nervously, Quinn walks through the front lobby of the hotel, clutching the room key like the sacred Sword of Omens. He wanders around the corner and finds the elevator. Though he forgoes eye contact, he shares a lift with a family of four, each dressed in bathing suits, having just come from the pool.

As they rise above the ground floor in the glass tube, the father turns to his young son and asks him, "You ready for Guardians tomorrow?"

"Yeah!" the excited boy replies. "Can't wait!"

Everyone disembarks at the third floor, though Quinn walks left in the opposite direction of the four vacationers. Midway down the corridor, he finds room 316. The door is slightly ajar. Quinn takes a few short, calming breaths, then attempts to enter, only for the security chain to stop him in his tracks.

"Is that you, Quinn?" Erin's voice echoes from inside the room. "Yeah."

"Good. I can't just leave the door open for anyone, you know."

Erin slowly undoes the chain, knowing that he is listening with anticipation to the scraping sound. When the door is finally unlocked, she takes several steps back, expecting him to charge into the room. Surprisingly, he hesitates for a second. Not wanting to wait any longer, she announces, "I'm ready for you!"

Quinn is unable to curb his enthusiasm as he opens the door. Erin stands in front of the room's two queen beds, auburn hair loose and frizzy around her shoulders. His eyes are filled with wonder as he realizes she's clad in nothing but a pair of black panties and her recently purchased black scarf. It dangles over her massive tits while she stares wantonly at the stunned young man.

"Well, if it isn't the mighty Quinn!" Erin declares as she approaches him. "Bet you ain't seen nothing like me, huh?"

The door to room 316 slams behind Quinn as he strides with purpose towards her. His cock, once again hardening rapidly, acts almost like a beacon of light pulling him closer to his own unforgettable dark thrill ride.

"I like your scarf," Quinn mutters.

"Why, thank you," Erin replies in her bedroom voice. "It's made from an authentic Mexican serape. I've been told it's seventy-two inches *long* and nine inches *wide*."

She closes in on the now-trembling young man. The fabric of her garment grazes his blue polo shirt.

"I wonder, how long and wide are you, Quinn?"

Erin barely lets those words resonate before grabbing the ends of her scarf, throwing it over her head, and slipping it around Quinn's waist, pulling him in tight to her body. She smirks as she tugs harder on the ends of the accessory, trapping his arms inside of it. His mouth hangs agape as he stares down at Erin's phenomenal bare breasts, and he starts panting deeply.

"This scarf is my new favorite article of clothing, Quinn," she continues before her eyes wander down to the bulge in his khaki shorts. "Mmm, I guess it's your favorite, too," she jokes.

"Holy cow!" he yells, wanting desperately to free his arms and relieve himself of his own garments.

Erin proceeds, even sultrier than before. "I can wrap it around my neck for added warmth," she says. "I can drape it across my shoulders, tie it around my throat... or I could tie *you* up and tease you until you explode!"

Quinn releases a distressed moan as precum escapes from the tip of his dick. Not knowing whether to bury his face in Erin's breasts or plead for his freedom, he opts to bend down to suck on her nipple, caught in sheer delight.

"Oooh, okay, Quinn," a surprisingly turned-on Erin remarks. "I'll let you out to play."

Releasing her scarf, she allows him to hastily remove his shirt, shoes, and shorts. Erin slyly shimmies her underwear down and off her body. As the eager young man goes for his boxers, she cuts him off, backing him up into a seated position at the foot of the bed closest to the door. An elated yet puzzled Quinn looks up at the nude masterpiece of a woman.

"What do you want to do, Miss Erin?" he asks.

She swiftly presses down on his chest and leans over him, her demeanor noticeably sterner.

"The first thing I want to do is set the record straight," Erin advises with conviction. "You do *not* call me Miss Erin. That title is reserved for one *special* man, not you."

Quinn's face further dissolves into thorough confusion. Quickly, Erin realizes her mistake in overestimating his mental capacity. She resets and assuages his ego to get what she truly wants from him.

"But don't worry," she adds, smiling brightly. "You're special, too, mighty Quinn. That's why I chose you for this occasion. I'm glad you came... Or at least, I'm glad you *will* be cumming."

With his self-esteem once again inflated, she nods, encouraging him to slide towards the headboard. When he obliges, Erin follows him onto the bed, deftly removing his boxers. His rigid five inches is rather unimpressive, yet she still feigns joy for the purpose of achieving her own pleasure.

"I bet you were hard from the moment I walked over to you, Quinn," she theorizes.

"Yes!" he answers honestly.

"I figured. I have that effect on people." Erin pauses, then adds, "I won't call you after tonight, but for now, you can call me... Miss Black."

Guiding her hands onto his thighs, she hovers over his manhood. Without warning or hesitation, Erin slides her mouth over his cock, methodically sucking it. Her hair flows over her head and grazes

Quinn's inner thighs, tantalizing him even more. Erin gently squeezes his balls for good measure.

"Oh, wow! Yes! Yes, Miss Black!" he exclaims.

Before long, his body trembles from Erin's masterful oral skills. With Quinn on the brink of release, she lifts her head and playfully massages his tip with her tongue.

He smiles and leans back as Erin proceeds to finish him.

"Ohhh! MISS BLACK! OHHHH!" he yells wildly.

Quinn's whole body shudders as he bursts inside Erin's mouth. Rising up, she deftly licks her lips in a move that the young student, immobile from ecstasy, doesn't even notice.

Still in a state of bliss, Quinn slowly lifts his head to see Erin staring down at him.

"I had to do you first. I had to drain you of all that nervous energy," she says. "I hope you understand."

Mustering all of his depleted strength, Quinn leans up towards Erin, his face revealing sheer amazement.

"Miss Black... No one has ever done that for me before," he admits, his voice full of earnest appreciation.

Unable to hide her shock and awe, Erin smiles and gulps at his admission. She summons the courage to pose the obvious question at a moment like this.

"Wow! Um, so, I don't know how to ask you this, but was that your... first?"

Quinn hastily responds, "Oh, no! No! I mean... I had a girlfriend in high school. We just did, like, the normal thing."

Restraining her laughter, Erin raises her brow and crosses her arms like a schoolteacher demanding a suitable explanation.

"The normal thing?"

"Well, yeah. Just, you know... Missionary," he notes before exhaling and elaborating with a somber tone. "Twice."

"Twice, huh? Well, the third time's the charm."

A wide-eyed Quinn agrees wholeheartedly. "I don't think I can ever top that."

Instantly, Erin shifts her body towards Quinn's head. He begins to grin at the sight of her up close.

"I think you can," she replies, her voice returning to a sensual tone.

Erin leans against the headboard, using it to pull her body upright. Before Quinn knows what's happening, she positions herself over his head, her pussy looming magnificently in full view.

"You ever see one of these up close before?" she furtively inquires, her dimpled grin growing even wider.

Energy suddenly replenished, Quinn's jaw drops at the sight of Erin's womanhood.

"No!" he answers before retracting his statement. "I mean, yes! Holy fuck, yes!"

Giggling at his Freudian slip, Erin advises him of the impending delight that just hours earlier would have been inconceivable.

"Here it comes, mighty Quinn!"

Delicately, she lowers herself straight down onto his face. Stifled, excited groans echo through Erin's body as she wriggles gleefully. Unsure of what to do, Quinn instinctively extends his tongue and hopes for the best.

"You like that?" she cunningly inquires, giving him a knowing look. "Oooh, that's right. You catch on quick."

Briefly, Erin spreads her thighs apart. Not wanting to completely smother Quinn, she lifts up her body to check on him. Her elated companion responds without hesitation.

"More! Please, Miss Black!" Quinn implores, his cock already reemerging from its post-ejaculation refractory period.

"You think you can find it?"

Initially uncertain how to answer but desperate to continue, Quinn begs Erin to proceed letting him devour her.

"Yes, I'll find it. I'll do anything."

Genuinely happy with his unbridled zeal, Erin obliges him and presses down on his face once again. After a few awkward seconds, the proverbial blind squirrel catches the nut, extending his tongue into Erin's pink wonderland, which makes her quiver.

"Ooooh, yeah, that's the stuff," she says as she wriggles on top of him. "Keep going. More, baby!"

Quinn presses his hands against the backs of Erin's quads and deepens his tongue, further burying his face inside of her. Erin clasps her breasts and plays with her nipples to increase her pleasure.

"Ohhh, yes! Yes!" she exclaims. "Almost there, baby!"

Quinn plunges deeper inside Erin with every ounce of energy he has and every inch of his tongue. She accentuates his efforts by writhing along with him. Her pussy wet and throbbing, Erin moans wildly which only makes Quinn more ferocious. Sensing the end is near, she arches her back and vigorously grabs her nipples.

"Ohhhh, yes! Yes, I'm cumming, baby!" Erin screams. "Yes!"

Shaking and trembling, Erin inadvertently squeezes Quinn's head, eliciting a groan of discomfort from her young partner. His pain is short-lived though. The power of her orgasm pushes her slightly backwards as her pleasure juices cover Quinn's mouth. Rolling onto her back, the proof of Erin's joy puddles on his cheeks and neck. Quinn touches his glistening skin with sheer curiosity and smells his fingers. His eyes widen in complete amazement, and he slips his ring finger inside his mouth, becoming more aroused.

"I can't believe it," he whispers softly.

Exhaling, Erin sits upright and glances over at Quinn, fully erect and throbbing once again.

"Are you referring to that," she gestures at his cock, "or my little squirt?"

Laughing, Quinn declares with glee, "Both!"

Like a serpent, Erin rolls over and fiendishly hovers over his dick. After a second of contemplation, she thinks of a clever way to finish him.

"I'm not surprised at your sudden resurgence," she declares. "But riddle me this. What's the fifteenth letter of the alphabet?"

Not allowing Quinn an opportunity to respond, Erin playfully widens her eyes, presses her thumb and index finger against the shaft of his penis, and strokes upwards, flicking his tip.

"O? OHHH!"

She repeats this method four times before Quinn arches his back. Erin casually leans away as his body judders and shoots a second load that coats his pelvis.

Delighted with her ability to please him, as well as herself, she leans in towards the motionless Quinn.

"I just love that second go-round where you completely drain someone," she informs him while kissing his cheek. "Oh, by the way, that's correct."

Quinn gathers his last remaining ounce of energy to reply, "I. Can't. Believe it."

"You're a great kid," Erin replies. "This was fun!"

Leaning up once again, he reiterates his previous statement and elaborates. "I've never seen anything like what you just did. It's... I don't even have words."

"That good, huh?"

"Fuck yeah!" Quinn confirms. "That's... I mean, Miss Black, that is the best sex I've ever had."

Erin genuinely smiles. "Well, thank you for the compliment."

Quinn sits up in the bed, his judgment clouded by passion, and asks hopefully, "You wanna grab a nice dinner for two?"

Erin laughs heartily, stands up, and proceeds to use the bathroom, finding her underwear in the process. Afterwards, she walks towards her neatly folded bra, shirt, and pants resting on top of the dresser. A dumbfounded and forlorn Quinn watches her gather her belongings.

"Let's not ruin a good thing, okay?" she reasons. "I got what I wanted. You got the best fuck you've ever had. I told you, I'm not calling you. This is done."

A genuine sadness washes over Quinn's face as he gets up to redress. He finishes buckling his belt, then turns to Erin wishing she would reconsider.

"I know what you said when we were, you know, in the moment," he tries. "I guess I was hoping maybe I could change your mind."

Realizing her attempts to blow him off are not going according to plan, Erin sighs and tries to explain her way of thinking to the oblivious Quinn.

"Someday, you'll figure out how this whole thing works," she counters. "Until then, take solace in the fact that you closed the deal with the hot girl. Face it, you've locked in a core memory here tonight."

Quinn gazes at Erin with longing. His expression is the textbook definition of bittersweet. With unyielding resolve, she places her hand on his shoulder.

"Something tells me the right one for you isn't going to sit on your face on the first date," Erin advises. "If we ever meet again, you'll thank me."

The UCF student laughs, then says his goodbyes and starts to exit. Before he opens the door to leave, Erin's voice stops him.

"Hey!" she calls out, waiting for Quinn to turn his head. When he does, she motions for him to come back. He gladly accommodates her, so Erin wraps her arms around him and delivers a warm, genuine embrace.

"Thank you, Quinn."

Quinn does not respond with words, but with a kiss on Erin's cheek. He then leaves without the girl, but with a whirlwind of emotions instead. As he reaches the elevator and walks into it, he begins to comprehend what Erin meant. Despite it all, he'd achieved what he set out to accomplish.

Subtly, Quinn pumps his fist as the doors close and he descends to the first floor. She was right about another thing, too. He will surely remember this day for years to come.

Back in room 316, Erin feels a cathartic sense of fulfillment in her own right. Not only did she satisfy her carnal desires, but through Quinn, she firmly believes she has exercised her demons.

Adrian's Hair Salon has an unlikely cancellation for five o'clock on a Tuesday evening, a welcome development for Erin Gillies. Recently returned from Florida, she walks into the Sterling, Virginia-based establishment for the first time. She finds a seat and waits for Shannon, the level three stylist tasked with remaking her appearance.

While she's waiting, she receives a text from her favorite Ashburn resident.

Hello, Miss Erin. I liked your personal video. I've been thinking about you. Can I see you this weekend?

The woman who has always possessed unmatched restraint finds herself melting yet again at the mere sight of his name on her phone.

"Bryce," she softly mouths before typing her response.

Hello, Mister Bryce. I'm not surprised. I seem to have that effect on people. Give me a time and place.

She sends the text and tries unsuccessfully to stop her mind from racing. With all the events from the past weekend lingering in her thoughts, for the first time, she does not merely want to focus on having sex with him. Although carnal pleasures are still her primary objective, Erin realizes she wants to have an honest conversation with Bryce.

Friday night. 6pm. Your place this time?

Before she can even process his last words, Shannon abruptly appears and greets her.

"Hi! Erin?" she asks.

"Oh, yes. Hi, I'm Erin."

Rising from her chair, she shakes Shannon's hand, extending the expected formality. Taken aback at the color and overall health of Erin's hair, Shannon can't help but confirm what has been requested.

"You have such a beautiful red," she remarks. "Are you sure you want the blank canvas?"

Undeterred, Erin emphatically nods. "I need a change. Change is good."

"Alright then," counters Shannon. "Black number one it is. The darkest we've got."

"Yup."

As they walk over to the sink to begin the process, a distracted Erin blurts out, "I hope he likes it. He's never seen me as anything other than a redhead."

The revelation is sudden, and Erin gasps surprised at herself. Her heart beats vigorously, and she wonders if she truly values Bryce's opinion or if she simply hopes he will still find her attractive afterwards.

"Oh. Husband or boyfriend?" asks Shannon.

Erin pauses and tries to choose her next words carefully. "None of the above... Well, not yet anyway."

Not yet? Erin yells at the demons in her head. *Not yet? No. Not ever. Remember the rules. Just sex.* Panic begins to set in. Anxiously, Erin sits in the chair and leans her head back over the sink, trying in vain to center her breathing.

"Relax, hun. I've got you," Shannon assures her, sensing her client's uneasy body language. "We can always change it back if it doesn't work for you. This is what we do. I promise — you're going to look even more ravishing as the woman in black."

Erin's eyes gradually exhibit a newfound sense of calm, and her mouth forms a devilish smile. *The woman in black.* Erin concludes that perhaps a physical change will encourage her to remain committed to keeping a strictly casual relationship with Bryce. With one last peaceful exhale as a full-fledged redhead, she replies with steely determination.

"I sure as hell will."

Episode Four: The Unaliving

1) Martha, My Dear

I'll never forget my mother. Irene Henning had a heart of gold and the voice of an angel. She loved The Beatles almost as much as she loved me, which is why she chose to name me Martha. I had my own song. There was no "Twinkle, Twinkle, Little Star" or "Soft Kitty" in my world. *Martha My Dear* was *my* lullaby.

Irene's maternal instinct was second to none. Even in the middle of the night when she was lost in the throes of sleep, she somehow knew when I needed her.

Whenever I'd awaken and scurry into the bathroom, she would appear. Like a ghost, she emerged out of the darkness. No creaking old wood floors, no audible footsteps announced her arrival. It was as though the sounds of my heaving and retching seemingly rose the undead. Her sixth sense was uncanny. Despite it all, she was just there.

In fact, my last fond memory of my mother comes from a time when I was near death. Ironic, isn't it? We are born from dirt, and we all return to it, some faster and more violently than others.

Stricken with measles, I'd spiked a fever of one hundred and five. Reality warped around me. My eight-year-old brain swore my bedroom was spinning and sinking into the earth.

Yet, Irene did not hesitate, nor did she waver. Confused and miserable, I tried to push her away. With the fire and fury of a mother determined to walk through *Dante's Inferno* rather than lose her only child, she force-fed me aspirin on a rigid schedule, practically shoving three or four capsules at a time down my swollen throat, then straddled me and dumped ice cold water into my mouth to chase them. I kicked and screamed like any child would, sobbing uncontrollably until the inevitable fatigue set in.

Finally, when I was too drained to fight her any longer, my mother scooped me into her arms and cradled me, clutching me tightly to her chest. Kissing my burning forehead ever so lightly, she rocked me back and forth, singing those words made famous by John Lennon and Paul McCartney. As the sickly girl that I was, I couldn't even hold my head up to listen. So, Irene carefully rested it in her arms and serenaded me.

My mother taught me how to tie my shoes and ride a bike. She helped me with my homework and played 'Tea Party' with me. No one has ever cared for me as much as she did in those precious moments. My mother was my everything.

For all those highlights, though, there were numerous lowlights, too. Few children my age had seen what I'd seen. Most kids were preoccupied with their gaming systems, their dolls and action figures, or worse, their baseball card collections. They didn't harbor visions of their drunken fathers throwing their mothers against the wall as I did.

Time after time, my father tortured Irene. Regularly, he punished her for his own personal shortcomings. He made sure to whip her where the marks could be hidden: upper arms, quads, the backs of her legs right below her ass cheeks. This was standard practice, carried out by the disgustingly vile Stan Henning.

Still, my mother was strong. She endured. Irene never let on how much he broke her spirit, not even the few times I flat out asked her about it.

"Why did Daddy beat you?" I inquired. "Were you a bad girl?"

"Oh no, my dear Martha. We were just playing."

Even my childlike brain recognized the blatant lies for what they were. I knew Stan was a monster, but that's the way it was - our broken family. We were simply my mother, myself, and Stan, the scum of the Earth. Irene never had a husband, and I never had a father. We had a cruel jailer.

Long before he met his maker, I decided I'd only call him "Daddy" out of obligation. He never expressed one iota of concern for me. He was never there for me when I was healthy nor when I was sick. I wasn't a boy, so to him, I didn't exist.

Once, I heard my mother meekly request Stan go to therapy to seek help with his penchant for drinking and violence. As soon as she finished speaking, Stan shot her a look. That was all it took. For a good five seconds, he stared her down as if to say, 'Don't you dare suggest that again.' Tension hung in the air for the rest of the evening.

That night, when I said goodnight and went to my room, there were no innocent bedtime stories. Instead, an audible smack and the pleas of a weeping young woman haunted my dreams.

In the days that followed, I did my best to play the innocent little girl, hoping he would not treat me with similar disdain. I played quietly in front of the TV while he laid on the couch with a beer in his hand until I finally worked up the courage to speak. Humbly, cautiously, I asked, "Why did Mommy want you to go to therapy?"

With a cold stare, Stan slowly put his beer bottle down and leaned in towards me. Unsure of his next move, I sat there frightened, not moving a single muscle lest it provoke him.

"Now, I'm only going to say this one time, little Martha," he sternly warned. "Therapy is *not* for you. Those people you see claiming they need counseling or AA? They all have fragile egos, weak minds, and soft bodies."

Suddenly, Stan pointed his finger at me. His next words were not so much fatherly advice as they were a threat.

"You will *never* need therapy or a support group to get through life. If you do, you will have lost all respect for yourself. Worst of all, you will have lost *my* respect."

I sat in stunned silence before turning back towards the TV. Terrified of what his next move might be, I slowly stood up and ran into the bedroom where my mother laid, reading a book. I asked her to have another tea party. Of course, she obliged. We both needed to be as far away from Stan as possible.

I couldn't even fathom what life would have been like for me if he hated me as much as he hated Irene. After all, as far as he was concerned, it was her fault he drank himself out of the minor leagues, never climbing higher than Double-A. She was also the reason he lost his job as the line cook at the diner – twice.

Truth was, his failures had nothing to do with Irene. Stan was always making reckless decisions. Not my mother. While she was by my side, he was out running the streets. My mother was the kind of woman who risked her life to nurse me back to health, but Stan was too busy drinking himself into oblivion.

But it wasn't the measles that took her in the end. A week after my fever finally broke, my life was set ablaze. Ten inches of snow covered all of Otsego County. Of course, that didn't keep Stan from driving to the Triple Play Tavern on a dark, frigid December night. Like always, he closed down the bar, despite no longer having a credible, steady income. On his way back home, the inebriated son of a bitch crashed his car into the metal fence in our driveway.

Of all things, that was the straw that broke my mother's back. You'd think she would have lost it over something more egregious, but I guess bottling up her anger for so many years finally took its toll. Enraged, she ran outside and chewed out her pathetic excuse for a husband. Seemingly caught off guard, Stan pleaded with her not to make a scene, to continue the conversation inside.

Irene obliged. Big mistake.

Once they were behind closed doors, Stan unleashed a fury like neither of us had ever seen. Even when he was sober, he was not above beating her senseless. This time, at his most intoxicated, he was determined to kill her.

Wide awake and scared for my life, I hid in my room, away from his drunken rage. As I cowered, I heard his fist connect with my mother's face three times, followed quickly by her head crashing into the wall. My ears rang as I waited for her screams, but they never came. Instead, I heard Irene gasping and choking. Sobbing, I cracked my bedroom door open, hoping my presence would stop the violence.

But it was too late. There was no hope and no escape.

Within minutes, the house fell silent. Shaking like a leaf, I slowly edged my way out into the hall. What I saw made *me* gasp and beg for air. The familiar sound of the disconnected landline screeched from the discarded receiver. On the floor beside the phone lay Irene, breathless and still.

My mother had been a saint. Now, she was soaring with the angels, far away from this putrid excuse of a human being. The one who stole her life, who took her from me.

It was then that something broke inside of me. I felt strangely detached. My brain had successfully "cleared the mechanism." The shrill beeping of the disconnected phone bypassed my senses, fading into my subconscious. A peculiar calm blanketed my anger. Numbness set into my limbs.

At first, Stan sat motionless in the corner of the living room. I couldn't tell if he was in shock or if a strange euphoria had overtaken him, but whatever emotions ran through his psychotic, murderous mind kept him from hearing me slink into the kitchen. I opened the drawer, and grabbed the biggest, sharpest knife I could find.

As I heard Stan slowly walk towards the phone, I crept around the corner behind him. I watched as he meticulously unwrapped the telephone cord from around my mother's neck.

Like the stone-cold killer that he was, Stan casually dialed 9-1-1, completely unaware of my presence. With a steely determination, I waited for him to turn around and face me. He wouldn't get the satisfaction of lying to the dispatcher about the sequence of events that led to Irene's death. He wouldn't get away with his abuse again.

When his fingers finished dialing, he spared me a glance. I was but a child, yet somehow, I possessed the strength and fervor of the devil herself. Like an apex predator, I went into my windup, ready to unleash hell upon him.

Even when sober, Stan never could hit a fastball, or so my mother had claimed.

Turns out, she was right. My knife sailed through the air, and a perfect strike pierced through his heart. Red justice was served before he even had time to swing.

I was judge, jury, and executioner, watching with sheer delight as he convulsed. He staggered to his feet and stumbled down the hallway. Everywhere he touched, the walls were streaked with the devil's work.

Stan Henning was out, once and for all. He was the first man I ever killed.

Before I knew it, the sound of splintering wood shot through the house as the cops burst through our front door. Heavy boots and radio static resonated and made me tremble in fear. From the living room, a female officer bellowed out, "Holy shit!" followed by "Holy Fucking Shit!" and "Code 5-3. Double homicide." Her radio crackled as she relayed the information back to base.

Moments later, a young male officer, whose nametag read E. Blackwood, slowly pulled back the covers. He found me alone, crying hysterically in my bed, where I'd hidden when the red and blue lights descended upon our driveway.

"Sam!" he shouted down the hall. "There's a girl in here!"

Turning towards me, he softened his stance and cautiously approached. I heard him murmur "Oh, Jesus!" I could only surmise the sight of the fresh splatter of blood on my cheeks and arms shook him to his core. Perhaps, he was simply expecting to break up a shouting match between a drunken, onery former athlete and his abused wife. Now, he found himself smack dab in the middle of a murder scene.

"What's your name, Miss?" he asked warily.

With a peculiar mix of fear and conviction, I kicked away what remained of my comforter and answered him. "Martha…" I sniffed. "Henning…"

"Officer Gladden!" he yelled as he, too, withdrew his radio and spoke into it. "Code 5-3, Double homicide. Need backup. Here with Officer Gladden at the Henning residence on Seminary Road. I have a juvie survivor, female, about eight or nine, name of Martha Henning. Need detectives ASAP for questioning."

A few seconds later, the female officer came storming down the hall. Her shadow darkened the doorframe where she lingered.

"I'll handle this, Ernie," she advised, before glancing back at the crime scene. "You take care of that. It's ugly."

Ugly. Welcome to my world, I thought.

Officer Gladden approached the bed and sat on the mattress. Guarded, she confirmed my identity. "You're Martha Henning? Daughter of Stan Henning?"

What a terrible fate bestowed upon me. The last thing I needed at that moment was to be lumped together with that expired piece of shit. Alas, he was known around town for his alleged baseball prowess, and my mother was not, so of course, I belonged to him.

"Yes."

From that moment on, it was all a blur. I didn't dare look into the hall. I'm sure Officer Gladden asked me a thousand questions. To this day, I don't remember a word of what I uttered. Our interaction is lost to history, forever suppressed.

All I know is that two homicide detectives arrived to discuss the ungodly events that had unfolded. I sat through their interrogation, wiping away my tears with blood-stained fingers. Eventually, one of the suited agents led me out of the house and into the back seat of a squad car.

For a time, everything was okay - until it wasn't.

Fingerprints don't lie, and mine were all over the murder weapon. Fortunately, a few things worked in my favor.

First, there was my tender age of eight and the earnest doctors who claimed my response was just. They cited neuroscience research which showed a child's decision-making abilities are not fully developed until they reach eighteen.

Then, there was Stan's reputation as an alcoholic. Sure, alcoholism doesn't necessarily equate to domestic violence, but it seemed he wasn't quite as adept at keeping secrets as he'd believed. People around town saw signs that there was trouble in paradise. The way he whispered to my mother in public and the way he often looked at her with scorn did not go unnoticed. Of course, this was only heresy in lieu of an actual police file. Maybe if one or two of them had spoken up instead of spreading rumors, they could have changed my mother's fate.

In the end, my punishment wasn't so severe. Still, the cold, harsh reality of the detention hall gave me all the therapy I needed. It helped me strengthen my fragile mind. Sadly, the powers-that-be also required I attend real counseling, the one thing Stan insisted I never seek, lest I lose my "self-respect."

Of all the times I ignored his so-called "advice," I took those words to heart. Therapy was for the weak. I hated it. After a few months, I learned to tell the counselors what they wanted to hear. In their minds,

I had learned the error of my ways. To them, murder was wrong. The only problem was those therapists didn't exist in *my* world.

Then again, my world had forever shifted. I had no home to go back to. No loving mother to hold me through my fears. There was only emptiness where my innocence once lived.

For several years following my release, I lived with Irene's mother, Gloria. She was kind and treated me like the world owed me a living. After everything that had happened, who's to say it didn't? Gloria attempted to fill the void. She showed me love and affection. I tried to reciprocate, but it felt strange. Deep down, even the idea of hugging her was awkward. I knew that was what other people did, but I wasn't like them. Besides, the last woman I showed any affection towards ended up dead.

Unlike Stan, Gloria didn't go out of her way to lay down the law. She wasn't a jailer. She wanted to play the "good cop" in my life, so she gave me freedom. All she asked of me was to call her when I went out after school and to be home by nine, not that I wanted to be with other people for that long anyway.

Once I reached high school, I heard about the football players working out in the fitness center. That's when it hit me: I needed to gain some muscle to strengthen my body like they did. Irene was a beautiful but dainty young woman. Perhaps if she were more physically gifted, she could have fought back against her disgusting husband. She might have lived.

Thus, I insisted on lifting weights. I ran track in high school simply to gain access to the gym after hours, and by the age of seventeen, I'd morphed into a five-foot-ten physical marvel – a strong, fast thoroughbred.

For a hot minute, I thought maybe sports could be my free ticket into college. When I reluctantly asked the track coach, Mr. Spano, about my options, he stared at me like a deer in headlights before answering.

"You're plenty fast, Martha, but you're becoming too, uh, *big* for cross-country," he finally said. "Have you considered a different path? Maybe powerlifting, or perhaps judo?"

Just another example of men treating me like a second-class citizen. Maybe he'd heard about that unfortunate incident when the star wide receiver, Jamal Sanders, thought he could take me in arm wrestling. It's too bad he was wrong. That put a damper on his season. You can't catch a ball from the sidelines with your arm in a sling.

Someone later told me his challenge was his way of trying to get to know me better. No dice. I wasn't interested. As far as I was concerned, to know me was to fear me. I told myself no man would ever weasel his way into my life. No one would hold that kind of power over me. I learned from my mother what not to do.

As I readied myself for college, I decided social interaction wasn't for me. My distance was for their own good as well as mine, as poor Jamal could attest. So, I broke down and went to my guidance counselor. That word: *Counselor*. It made me sick to my stomach.

Nonetheless, I sucked it up and walked into his office unannounced. He'd never seen me before. I'm sure he feared me from the moment he saw me, and rightly so.

With a pensive demeanor, he cautiously asked, "How may I help you?"

"Hi. I'm Martha Henning."

Attempting to break the ice, he leaned back in his chair. "Martha, my dear. I'm a huge fan of the Fab Four, you know."

That was strike one. I was not his *dear*. I was no one's dear. Not anymore. Yet, I stood there and told him, point blank, "I don't like people. What can I do with my life?"

Taken aback by the way I'd bluntly negated small talk, his eyes darted around the room.

"Well, let me pull up your report card, Miss Martha."

Strike Two. I was nobody's "miss," either. As I stared at him, my mind fueled my body with fury and venom. I decided to give him one more chance before the pathetic, misguided middle-aged loser learned a swift, hard lesson of his own.

"Your math scores are off the charts. Have you considered an accounting program?" the counselor offered. "There are plenty of SUNY schools to choose from if you're interested."

Before he had a chance to say or do anything to further deter his career, I thanked him and walked out without a backwards glance. From there, I found the nearest bathroom and vomited in the first toilet I saw.

As senior year progressed, Gloria graciously offered to pay for my judo classes. She saw it as an opportunity for me to get out and meet boys. Fuck that. I saw it as an opportunity to learn how to end boys should they ever attack me the way Stan did to Irene.

I applied to four different schools, none within the state of New York. Three accepted me. I chose the one farthest away – the University of Richmond.

On my eighteenth birthday, I also changed my name. Martha Henning was tainted. She was a murderer with a past no one would wish on their worst enemy. She'd seen the devil incarnate and felt her coursing through her veins.

I chose Heather Berard as my new identity. It sounded strong and immaculate, just like me. Gloria didn't feel it was necessary, but she reluctantly went along with it. She said she understood my decision and wanted me to find peace. There was no peace to be made, but at least no one could say Heather was a killer.

It pained me to give up my song, the namesake my mother had granted me, but it was necessary. Heather Berard would surely begin her adulthood with a clean slate. I swore on Irene Henning's lonely grave that Martha was dead and gone.

But some promises are made to be broken. I couldn't have been more wrong.

2) Peaks Allure

You'd think I would have discovered my body and the male response to it well before I became old enough to vote. Believe it or not, that wasn't the case. I was too self-absorbed in high school, too intent on making myself stronger, and while boys had no clue about my past, they were wary of my reputation. Most stayed at arm's length.

Forget prom. I'd never even kissed a boy back in Cooperstown, but in college, I made up for lost time. Not because I wanted to. Opportunity came knocking. I soon found out that the best way to beat a young man was to get in his pants.

It started with a few curious glances. Every once in a while, I'd catch some poor, hormonal primate staring at me in class. When I turned my head towards them, they would immediately look away. After a while, I saw their eyes trailing down my arms and boring through my shirt with immeasurable curiosity.

Well, *almost* immeasurable. More than once, I caught glimpses of their unruly erections as they pretended to listen intently to lectures about current events and the impact social media has on setting the narrative. Let's just say I became a distraction.

I couldn't fathom why until some anime fan named Charles Sinclair, who sat next to me in Economics class, awkwardly leaned over towards me. When I abruptly stared him down, Charles raised his hand, barely able to spit out a coherent question.

"Heather, right? Are, uh... Are you cosplaying?" he innocently asked.

I had no idea what he was referring to, so I became defensive. No, I became *offensive*, straightening my body upright and quickly balling my fists.

"What?" I barked at him.

A shaken Charles began rocking slowly. He diverted his eyes towards the floor, then reached into his backpack and retrieved his DVD copy of the adult anime film, *Votor's Throne*. He flipped the case around to show me the back. To my surprise, a black-haired, scantily clad goddess stared back at me. Her physical features were unmistakable: huge muscles, massive breasts, and defined abs. She was a masterpiece. The perfect woman.

"Peaks Allure," Charles said. "She's Votor's bodyguard. She flexes and makes her tits bounce."

I stared at the case with increasing curiosity. "Hmm, so, she can make her tits bounce, huh?" I asked.

"Um, yeah..."

Chuckling softly, I looked down at my own rack. Without hesitation, I flexed my boobs up and down in unison. Charles immediately smiled and cackled as my boobs danced underneath my black t-shirt.

"Oh my God. Yes!" he exclaimed, rising from his chair. "That's amazing. You *are* her! The resemblance is uncanny."

"So I am," I cooed. "Tell me more about this Peaks Allure."

After a brief hesitation, Charles relayed her origin story. "She was abandoned as a child and abused as a teenager. Votor saved her from a life of prostitution. He's the main character, you know... Well, anyway, his family disowned him and his friends betrayed him because he took pity on this girl, so he went on a mission to reclaim his kingdom. He started the Strike Force."

Nodding in acknowledgment, I let him finish the story of my alleged doppelganger.

"Peaks Allure decided to become this mighty physical specimen to avenge her past. She could kick ass or she could seduce them first, then beat them. She's got *guns* for arms. But, yeah, her flexing and titty bouncing is, like, her secret weapon. It makes the men super hard, and the women super wet, too. Like, *everyone* wants her. Peaks distracts her adversaries, gets them all to lower their defenses, and then BAM! They're done."

Surveying my body and comparing it to hers, I suddenly realized the woman on the case was truly my mirror image. Thanks to Charles, for the very first time, I acknowledged the power I truly possessed.

"She puts Bond villains to shame," he advised.

With a wry smile, I took the DVD case and read the description on the back. Finished, I casually pressed the case against Charles's stomach. To my wondering eyes, his own "peak" started to form as he nodded awkwardly. His cheeks flushed red, and I heard a very faint "uh" escape his lips.

"I guess that makes me Votor's Strike Force, huh?" I furtively replied. I walked away from that exchange with a newfound under-standing of how to defend myself if needed. Lure them in, then take advantage of them. Judging by Charles' reaction, it wouldn't be that hard to manage.

With that in mind, you'd think I'd know better than to date an athlete of all things.

Yet, most of my free time was spent at the gym during my freshman year. After my serendipitous exchange with Charles, I started noticing male jocks staring at me even more. They truly marveled at my physical prowess.

On more than a few occasions, some rando walked over to me in the middle of my reps. Their segues were predictable, always something along the lines of, "Hey, are you a female wrestler?"

Either they couldn't fathom that I was an accounting major with no real interest in playing sports or they simply needed an attitude adjustment. Not wanting to repeat the Jamal Sanders incident unless provoked, I swallowed my desire to make mincemeat out of them and answered accordingly.

"Yes, I'm a female, and if you want to wrestle, you'll lose," I promised. That sent them scurrying off fast.

Then, there was Bobby Downing, who seemed nice enough for a testosterone-fueled young man. I was four months into my freshman year when he approached me one day while I was on the bench press. He watched in awe, all six-foot-one and two hundred fifteen barrel-chested pounds of him, eager to learn a few tricks of the trade.

"Man, if I had your biceps, I'd be a high draft pick for sure," he uttered.

Abruptly, I racked my weights, sat up and turned around. His smile was wide and silly. He appeared captivated. This was becoming quite the trend; had the men back home seen me in the same light all along?

Bobby stood there, frozen in time, hoping I wouldn't notice the small erection forming beneath his athletic shorts. Of course, I did, and I couldn't help but wonder to myself, *Who does this fucking goofball think he is?*

"Listen, Chubbs. If that's your best pickup line, you have bigger problems than getting drafted," I advised.

"Oh, no, no," he responded, taken aback. "I was just amazed by your body."

Sweat beaded on my tank top as I stalked towards him. With each step, his confidence quickly waned, giving way to nervousness.

"Clearly. Your amazement is written all over your dick," I mused. Immediately, he glanced down, bent over, and backed away in utter embarrassment.

"Oh! I'm sorry. I..."

"What sport do you play?" I asked, ignoring his apology.

Hesitantly, he quietly stammered. "Ba... Baseball."

At that moment, I could have easily dispatched him the way I did Jamal or sent him scurrying away with just a look of disdain. Then, I remembered Peaks Allure and her secret weapons. Perhaps this was the right time to test my mettle. Maybe it was time to see if I could really kill someone with kindness before discarding them.

Thus, I took pity on the poor, wretched fool. I figured I could use a guy like him, literally and figuratively. Sneering, I spared him an unfortunate trip to the orthopedist.

"Well, luckily, you only have *two* strikes, and I could use a spotter," I responded. "Are you going to do something about that, or are you just going to stand there?"

Gradually, I allowed Bobby into my life, or at least the life I led him to believe I had. I told him my parents died in a car accident when I was twelve and my grandmother took me in afterwards. At least that last part was accurate. Worst case scenario, if anyone ever met Gloria and she spilled the tea, I could privately explain it was bullshit. Maybe my grandmother never properly dealt with the trauma of losing her daughter and was starting to develop dementia. It was plausible.

Bobby was just a sophomore, but with my encouragement, he cracked the starting lineup. Not only did he start hitting like a four-year senior, but he was also named the Atlantic-10 Conference Player of the Week.

As Bobby and I officially became boyfriend and girlfriend, I figured he'd eventually want to have sex. So, I decided to practice on myself first. I bought a few toys and experimented. It was an eye-opening experience, to say the least. Plus, it came with the added benefit of popping my own cherry. No man could claim they'd taken it.

Once I was alone in my dorm room, I laid on my bed and inserted my vibrator for the first time. Yes, I was aware of the notion that women should begin slowly with a small dildo, plenty of lube, and no vibration, but I was no ordinary woman.

The pressure made my pussy ache, so I immediately removed it and stared at the thin coating of blood on the silicone. An innate curiosity grew inside of me. Despite the pain, curiosity urged me to forge ahead.

Boy, did I ever. Slowly, my silver toy entered my sex once again. The discomfort quickly gave way to pure, unadulterated pleasure. Moaning and groaning, my glorious body quivered incessantly, feeling weak and vulnerable. Yet, I smiled for the first time in so long. I finally understood what the rest of the world craved.

As I moved my vibrator around, I found my sweet spot and convulsed on my bed. My brain, wary of losing control, told me to stop, but my body begged me to give in to my desires. With no one to see me at the mercy of my pleasure toy, I listened to my body. I allowed myself a moment of sheer ecstasy. Before long, I felt my core explode in a cathartic moment of bliss.

Unable to withstand any more, I turned off my vibrator. As I laid there prone, my heavy breathing gradually morphed into raucous laughter. I wasn't sure at that moment what made me happier: the fact that I'd pleasured myself or the thought of knowing what I could really do to another man, understanding the power I could wield. I wanted nothing more than to savor the moment.

I then wondered what to do with my new male companion. How could I translate my orgasm to his? I'd procured a couple of pornos from the video store, so I turned on the DVD player and explored the sexual stylings of two well-schooled, nympho actors.

Then, in a moment of sheer curiosity, I switched over to *Votor's Throne*. After all, Peaks Allure was my alter ego, and I wanted to witness her in action. To my dismay, the opening sequence featured a much younger, less defined version of Peaks Allure being cornered and physically assaulted by an abhorrent man named Ridge Vallis, Votor's arch nemesis.

"Your sword is no match for mine," Ridge declared, gazing down at his erect cock. "Your strike force cannot save you, and your shield cannot stop me. Now, you will feel how big and powerful I truly am."

Though her harrowing origin was foretold, the animated images on the screen sickened me. It wasn't just the fact that my doppelganger was sexually abused. I couldn't shake this feeling that I'd seen and heard it all before.

As I stared at the screen, images raced through my mind, repressed memories of things my mother tried to hide. Suddenly, there I was, fighting through the fever. After Irene sang me to sleep, I woke up in the middle of the night. Sweating profusely, I stumbled out of bed and hugged the wall as I passed down the hall to use the bathroom. However, the sound of weeping halted me in my tracks.

"Please, Stan. Not tonight. I'm exhausted," my mother softly begged.

I didn't dare look into their bedroom. Something inside told me to wait, lest I face an unspeakable punishment. All I heard was Stan, undeterred and determined to have his way.

"I told you this was happening tonight," he growled.

"We can't. You'll wake her up," Irene replied, attempting to reason with an unreasonable man, unaware that I'd already risen from my slumber. "She needs to rest."

"Oh, I'm already awake, and I told you I wanted a son to carry on my legacy," he warned. "Now, open up or I'll make you open yourself up to me."

"No!"

Naturally, "no" meant "yes" to Stan.

The mattress creaked, and Irene began to cry. The sounds of my whimpering matched my mother's. Over and over, I heard her moan, though not with pleasure.

"That's right, Irene," Stan proclaimed, grunting in time with the headboard's rhythmic thumping against the wall. "Your glove cannot stop me. I have a big and powerful bat. Admit it, you love the force with which I *strike* you."

Later, it was time to show Bobby what I could do. I agreed to let him take my virginity, but not because I cared about him. The memory of Stan's aggression lingered in the back of my mind. Sex was a means to an end. The devil gave me breasts, and I gave myself a body to die for. If I was going to use my weapon, I needed to learn exactly how to get men off.

Fortunately, my lethal combination left Bobby harder than his aluminum bats. Ferociously mounting him, I writhed and rode him to glory. Surprised and aroused by my fervor, it didn't take Bobby very long to cum.

To be honest, it didn't take me long, either. My first real sexual encounter with a man was almost as good as that fine day alone in my dorm. I'll never forget those immortal words he uttered after he finished and collapsed beside me.

"You fuck like a porn star, Heather. I love it!"

For the next couple of weeks, I went through the motions. I opened myself up to him just enough to make him comfortable. Still, I didn't divulge anything truly personal, only things more along the lines of my favorite foods or places to visit.

It began to seem like we were a real couple. Over time, I started questioning my initial intention of using Bobby as a prop to further my own cause. I couldn't help but wonder, *Am I growing soft? Is this what love is truly supposed to be like?*

That all changed suddenly when he made one fatal mistake. He, too, invoked my past and triggered my defenses.

Like the good girlfriend I tried to be, I visited him at the indoor facilities one day after a game. Bobby was a determined athlete, insisting on practicing after he'd just played. He fixated on that pitching machine and made hard contact every time the ball fired towards him. When he stopped to say hello, I took that as my cue to step inside the batter box and tell him he'd played an excellent game.

I barely saw it coming. Like a shot from a cannon, a ninety mile-per-hour fastball careened at me. At the last moment, I turned to avoid the impact, which would assuredly have smashed my face. Instead, the ball clocked me on the side of my head.

They said I lost consciousness for about thirty seconds. The next thing I saw were doctors and trainers surrounding me, their overlapping voices asking me questions. My skull throbbed and nausea churned in my stomach. Bobby stood against the back of the cage, stone-silent, face flushed. At first, I backed away from everyone. The buzzing in my ears overwhelmed my compromised senses.

Finally, I grasped their most basic of inquiries: Who was I? Where was I from? Dazed and confused, I softly muttered "Martha," before quickly recanting my old name.

"No! Heather... Heather Berard from Cooperstown, New York," I mumbled.

Faintly, I heard Bobby laugh as my so-called significant other stepped forward and pretended to console me.

"Tell Martha to bring her glove next time," he joked. "Come on, let's get you to your feet."

Excuse me? Bring my what? You lured me into this cage, didn't you?

Despite my faux pas, a concussion was the easy diagnosis. The doctors swore my getting hit in the head with a fastball was a freak occurrence, but I knew better. I'd seen this trick before. All the proof I needed lay in a single suppressed memory, one in which Stan played "catch" with six-year-old Martha.

That disgusting, bottom-feeding, waste of space didn't have the will or the patience to teach me I should turn my hand out towards the ball instead of lifting my wrist to scoop it out of the air. One by one, each of his baseballs fell at my feet.

"Not like that! Like *this*!" he yelled.

When the following hard throw glanced off my glove, I ran after it. Little did I know the miserable drunk fuck had picked up another wayward ball. As I bent over to retrieve the one which had rolled away, Stan threw the new baseball as hard as he could and struck me in the back of the head.

Imagine that! A grown man, a so-called father, throwing at his six-year-old daughter's head. He tried to take me out, but he failed. I got the last word in the end. Stan received his comeuppance, even if it took him two years to meet his fate.

Some twelve years after Stan assaulted me, Bobby did the same, but he didn't even have the guts to take the credit. He knew the pitching machine would go off. Timed it just right. All along, he'd been lowering my shield by pretending to care for me. I was supposed to be manipulating him, yet *he* was the one who used sex as a means to an end. I fell for it, hook, line, and sinker.

Bobby was just like everyone else: a lying, scheming sack of shit. Now, he was about to get what he had coming to him.

My plan was two-fold. First, I had to break his heart, then I'd destroy his body. It was *my* turn to use sex and beat Bobby at his own game. I needed to find someone close to him, someone whom he trusted. Perhaps a teammate could be my muse.

So, I watched the Spiders practice, carefully scouting each player. Before long, I found a familiar face, a freshman third baseman named Bryce Palmieri.

Bryce was a shy kid with a six-pack and enough talent to warrant hanging around with a physical specimen like me. I also knew Bryce from Economics class, so I approached him under the guise of needing extra help.

Feigning innocence, I followed him back to his dorm room after practice. He said he needed to take a shower. All I really did was help him out of his sweaty t-shirt and toss it into his hamper.

Okay, I'll admit I *had* to touch his abs, too. I'd never actually felt a man with a rock-hard washboard stomach before.

When I looked down, Bryce was bulging. At first, I figured it was just his athletic supporter until I heard him groan and begin breathing heavily.

Shyly, he said to me, "I have to take this out. My... My cup."

I knew my assignment immediately. Without hesitation, I backed him up against his door and kneeled in front of him. With a devilish stare, I undid Bryce's uniform pants, reached inside his jockstrap, and playfully fondled him, pretending to grab his massive cock on accident.

"Oops," I chuckled, trying not to reveal my amazement at his size. "That's not what we're looking for."

"Oh my God!" he exclaimed. "Yes, it is!"

That was all I needed to hear. Slowly, I removed his cup, lowered his uniform pants and briefs, and used my total package to satisfy his. I began with oral, then opted to give him a better view of my glorious tits. I took off my shirt and unhooked my bra; the mere sight of my bare breasts made him twitch.

"I think we've figured out the concept of supply and demand," I deviously cooed. "But I may need help with my Russian homework instead."

Crouching down, I proceeded to give my new favorite ballplayer a nice titty fuck. Much like Bobby, it didn't take Bryce long to cry out and burst with joy.

When he finished, I smiled wickedly as I coolly rose to my feet. Walking over to his hamper, I took his discarded shirt and smirked like a she-devil as I separated my breasts and wiped away his cum with it. The look in his eyes slowly morphed from quivering astonishment to confident bliss.

"Heather," he exhaled. "That's never happened to me before."

Stunned, I could no longer stifle my laughter. "You mean you've never cum?"

"No, no," he amended. "I mean, I have, but I've always done it myself. No one's ever done it *for* me, not until now. And that... Wow, that was incredible."

Cheating on that scumbag Bobby with a teammate was satisfying enough for me. The fact that I was Bryce's first sexual experience just made me want him even more.

"Has anyone ever said you look like Peaks Allure?" he remarked.

With newfound purpose, I chuckled as I stood up nice and straight, giving him another good look at my dynamic duo. "So, I've heard."

With a fiendish grin, I bounced my tits over and over. Bryce's eyes became as big as saucers.

"Holy fuck! You *are* her!" he bellowed, swiftly rising to the occasion yet again.

"I sure am. You got enough left in that tank for some *real* action, Big Bryce?"

Spoiler Alert: He did. Our second time was glorious. Just like that, I'd executed my first trade. I exchanged that callous creep for a bigger, better, sexier boy toy.

Like the grown adult that I *wasn't*, I broke up with Bobby over text and showed up to practice arm in arm with Bryce the very next day. Naturally, my current and former partners had an altercation on the field not long afterwards. I was the reason.

Bobby was immediately kicked off the team for his aggression. I should have felt honored that two strapping young men would fight over me. Instead, I felt an overwhelming sense of satisfaction. Phase one was complete, and the result was better than even I expected. Not only was Bobby heartbroken, but he'd also lost his spot on the team.

Now, it was onto phase two. My eyes and ears told me Bobby would transfer to Western Carolina. I couldn't let that happen. He'd be out of my reach. I simply could not stand idly by and watch another Stan Henning materialize in our world.

Thankfully, I knew I could get to him. Before I ended our relationship, Bobby told me about his sister's upcoming wedding. It was taking place on Memorial Day weekend in Virginia Beach. They'd secured the large ballroom at the Rotunda Hotel, close to the boardwalk. Surely, he would have his own room, and there wasn't enough time for him to find another plus-one for the occasion.

Bryce was going home to Fredericksburg for the summer. I told him I was returning to New York, but we'd definitely see each other. Naturally, this warranted a little white lie to my grandmother. So, I pledged my love for Bryce and told her his parents were allowing me to stay with him for a couple of weeks before he started his summer job. The stage was set.

Bobby would never see me coming.

3) Twisted Steel and Sex Appeal

You never forget your first "unaliving," but much like my sex life, my second time was even better. The murder required a longer, more complex course of action, which made it all the more satisfying when my plan came to fruition.

The stars aligned perfectly on that beautiful, clear night. I showed up at the ocean front at ten-thirty, late enough that everyone was nice and tipsy. My black Jessica London single-breasted pantsuit with matching high heels and clutch said I was there for business, not for pleasure.

I was dressed for the occasion with matching black parade gloves to complete the ensemble. I may have omitted my white shirt, but surely, I wouldn't be needing it for long. Its absence would only help me end Bobby.

Since I hadn't been dating him for very long, and we'd only met at college, I wasn't on a first-name basis with any of the Downing family. The only one who would recognize me was the man himself. So, I strutted into the main lobby like I owned the place, and it didn't take long to locate my target. The barrel-chested loser was slumped over in the hallway outside of the reception hall.

As I studied him, my mind flashed back to that night in Cooperstown - the last time I'd seen my mother alive, the evening Stan came home hammered. For a brief moment, the bastard's face replaced my ex-boyfriend's. Rage boiled within me. How dare Bobby sear that image into my mind again when I'd tried so hard to bury it? The resurrected memory only strengthened the urge to carry out my mission.

As I blinked, the image before me cleared, and I once again saw my ex-boyfriend. Though he hadn't played in several weeks, Bobby was still in fine shape. However, he was heavily impaired. I was a lucid five-foot-ten, black-haired succubus, with one hundred and ninety pounds of muscle, tits, twisted steel, and sex appeal. And he... Well, he was easy prey.

An old, familiar presence entered my body as I stalked over to him. It was the same other-worldly sensation that had bolstered Martha until she was strong enough and vicious enough to kill Stan, only this time, I was ready for it. Vitality blossomed in my chest the closer I stepped towards Bobby. As our eyes met, I felt more than capable of burning one last core memory into his brain before his inevitable demise.

"Heather!" Bobby slurred happily, staring up at me with adoration. "I didn't think you were gonna make it!"

Casually smiling back, I played along, knowing full well I was in control of the game. I stooped to his level and returned his affection. "Oh, babe! I wouldn't miss this for the world," I informed him as I gently hugged him and kissed his cheek.

"Wait..." Bobby frowned with concern as one last ounce of clarity crept into his brain.

"I thought you broke up with me. Where's that punk, Bryce?" he wondered. He scanned the space in search of the other man before turning back to me.

Cupping the sides of his face, I deliberately tilted it down and delivered a sweet peck to his forehead. His eyes, swimming in alcohol, took a good, long look at my vast cleavage, which hovered at eye level.

"Oh, honey, trust me. Bryce was just a phase," I lied as I reached for his hands. "I've thought about what happened, and I made a mistake. I'm here for *you*, Bobby. Not him."

His heart raced as I leaned into him. Through the fabric of his slacks, I felt his dick growing, right then and there in public. Struggling to compose himself, Bobby gulped and tried to stand upright.

"Did you, uh, meet Rick and Liz?" he inquired, clutching the wall for support. "Oh! And my parents—"

"Yes!" I gleefully interrupted. "They're having the *best* time, and I want to show *you* the best time, too."

Allowing himself to become distracted, the robust object of my desire wrapped his arm around my waist, pulling me tighter to his chest. Wordlessly, Bobby's giddy smile confirmed he was all but mine for the taking.

"Well, I'm ready whenever you are." he offered with a sloppy wink. As though in afterthought, his eyes darted to the open ballroom doors where cheery guests danced the evening away. "Um, I should say goodbye..."

I quickly corrected him. "Oh, no! I already said goodbye for the both of us. They understand."

Sure enough, Bobby allowed me to lead him away.

A stranger watched us stride towards the elevator, arm in arm. As we passed, he patted Bobby on the shoulder as if to say, 'Nice score with the lady.'

Indeed, someone had scored that evening, but it certainly wasn't Bobby. Doing my best not to laugh, I gazed at "my man" as he pressed the 'Up' button. I'd already pressed his 'Up' button with ease. Anyone with half a brain could see the erection straining against his slacks. So, we left the guests behind when the doors slid open, the seemingly inconspicuous, picture-perfect couple heading off to enjoy our own festivities.

Slowly, the elevator doors closed, sealing us inside. For a moment, fear gripped my heart, causing it to thrash against my ribs. *Am I really going to do this?* I asked myself.

But as Bobby and I ascended to the sixth floor, an unmistakable song drifted from the speakers: *Martha My Dear*. Her song. *My* song, even if I had changed my name.

This was no coincidence. Here I was in the thick of it with Paul's dulcet tones escorting us to our final destination. My mother's presence filled the empty space surrounding us, both overwhelming and reassuring me. I knew then, for certain, this was fate.

"I'm right around the corner. First door on the left," he noted. He gave my hand a squeeze. We exited the elevator and made our way to room 606, Bobby barely managing not to trip over his own feet. "I'm so glad you came back, Heather. I really needed you here."

Almost feeling sorry for him, I leaned my head against his shoulder in a show of faux sympathy. "I'm glad, too. I'm not going anywhere, Big Bobby."

I stroked his back while he fumbled with his key trying to fit it properly into the slot. The irony didn't escape me. *That's always a problem for men, isn't it?* I thought, subtly shaking my head. He didn't notice.

Seductively, I reached in and deftly guided his card into the slot. With a click and a promise, I let him take the lead. He drew me into his room, shutting out the rest of the world. Little did Bobby know when this door closed, none would ever reopen for him again.

I wasted no time in giving him one last ride, spinning him around and kissing him with gusto. It took little effort on my part to guide him onto the king-sized bed. As he scooted towards the headboard, I pounced on him.

Bobby groaned with pleasure as I seated all of myself on top of him. Swiftly, I straddled him like a thoroughbred, undoing his blue tie and unbuttoning his shirt while grinding. His breath became laborious, unable to withstand my movements.

"I'm a little out of shape," he meekly remarked.

"Oh, don't worry," I replied. "You don't have to do anything, baby. I've got you covered."

My thighs gripped his sides, making his eyes bulge in wonderment. His breathing quickened, and his rod's length increased.

"Wow! You're stronger than I remembered," he noticed. "Guns and breasts."

Gleaming at him, I raised my eyebrows. "I'm strong in other ways, too," I taunted. "Let me remind you."

Bobby attempted to free his arms from his grey suit jacket, but I held them down and playfully shook my head.

"Oh no, big Bobby!" I retorted as I leaned in and teasingly kissed the bridge of his nose. "You don't move a muscle. You'll get your chance, but first, I need to make it up to you."

His fledgling abs heaved with delight practically begging me to acknowledge them. Instead, I glided my hands to his hips and undid his belt buckle. Not wanting to ruin the moment, he ceased trying to remove his jacket and watched me as I turned my gaze to his groin, licking my lips.

Bobby's rigid cock twitched, aching to be released from his pants. Of course, I didn't disappoint, quickly unfastening his button, then tugging on his zipper. Sliding his pants down to his ankles, I reached through the opening of his boxers to free him.

"Wow! Yes!" he exclaimed, as every man did. Then again, with all that blood flowing from his brain into his lower head, I could hardly blame him. Men were feeble creatures, easily driven to slaughter by their hormones and selfish natures.

As stiff as aboard, his hardly impressive five inches greeted me. *Hey, it's the thought that counts, right?* I internally scoffed at the sentiment. I knew it wouldn't take long to end him. I just had to give him exactly what he wanted. I guess Bobby had never heard the other common expression: "Be careful what you wish for."

With a devilish grin, I pinned his wrists against the bed and arched my back. Taking a deliberate, deep exhale, I wrapped my lips around his throbbing cock. Bobby grunted in ecstasy as I sucked him off with flawless precision. Each time I thrust down to the base of his shaft, he moaned. His audible groans grew louder and louder by the second. I'd barely begun my task and already, he was close to the edge.

Yes, I'm *that* good!

Ever so lightly, I scraped my lower teeth against the bottom of his member. This did the trick even sooner than I'd anticipated.

Suddenly, he belted out a resounding "UHHHHHH! WOW!"

Bobby's body vibrated violently on the bed. I let out a gentle "Mmmm" as I continued to consume him, making him think I wanted it as much as he did.

Sure enough, Bobby exploded in my mouth. The tremendous force and volume of his release once again surprised me, forcing me to back off ever so slightly as I swallowed his pleasure.

Finished, I sat up in the bed. Bobby remained limp and powerless beneath me, his heartbeat gradually slowing and his breathing steadying. It was then I made a startling discovery: I'd been so preoccupied with getting him off, I never even had to disrobe myself. All it took was one forced glance at my perky, tucked 44DDs and he was mine for the taking.

He was making it far too easy. Slipping off the bed, I stood up beside him, and opened my suit jacket.

"Well, Bobby Downing, I hope that was good for you," I furtively commented. In one fell swoop, I dropped my jacket to the floor, revealing the black lace bra underneath. Slowly, Bobby arched his neck and propped himself up on his elbows. His eyes widened, and his eager expression told me he wasn't quite finished.

"Fuck!" he roared.

With a sly grin, I replied, "Ha. Now, there's an understatement."

Casually, I reached over and pushed his upper body upright then slipped in behind him, allowing him to rest his frame against mine. Feigning innocence, I gently wrapped my thighs around his waist, ensnaring him.

Dreamily, Bobby wondered, "What are you doing now?"

Reaching around his torso, I pushed aside his open shirt and rubbed his pecs.

Then, I pressed my lips against the back of his neck at the collar of his wrinkled jacket.

"I just want to have a nice moment to cool down with my *boyfriend,*" I fiendishly answered. "Before I drain you *completely.*"

Laughing heartily, Bobby sighed and tilted his head back and to the left.

"I'm pretty well drained, I think," he chuckled. "Hey, what's with the gloves, by the way?"

"Oh? Are you sure about that?" I challenged, craftily avoiding his question. To further distract him, I began playing with his nipples. "Because I seem to remember a strapping young slugger who loved my big tits. He once came for me twice in one night. Yeah, Bobby! You're a mighty pull hitter with a big, powerful *wooden bat*, aren't you?"

Purposely, I let those words linger. I watched as, to my surprise, his other wooden bat, still glistening with cum, revealed itself once again. He was so easily manipulated. Such a shame. I'd miss him when I was finished. But I knew the moment of truth had arrived. I had to end this.

"Western Carolina would be *very* happy to have you," I said as I slowly breathed into his ear.

Preoccupied with his rising dick, Bobby didn't notice my right hand reaching around his neck and grabbing the lapel of his jacket. He was already dead; he just didn't know it yet.

With sudden, cat-like reflexes, I lifted his left arm, pinning it behind him with mine. Then, I pushed the back of his head down, using my right hand to strangle him with his own jacket. Simultaneously, I crushed his waist between my powerful thighs, trapping his other arm against his body. Before he knew it, he was immobilized. There was no escape from my reach.

Sarcastically, I added, "Oh, by the way, did I tell you I learned judo in high school?" Breathless, Bobby began flailing violently. "This," I remarked, squeezing a little tighter, "is a choke hold called Kata Ha Jime. It's Japanese for, 'You're fucked.' This particular move cuts off the oxygen supply to the brain."

Gasping for air that wouldn't come, Bobby desperately began tapping his right hand, begging me to release him.

Of course, I declined his request.

"Oh, no, big Bobby," I said, fire seeping into my tone. With sick and twisted resolve, I continued. "This isn't ultimate fighting. You can't tap out. This is *my* game, and it ends when you stop breathing."

Terrified, Bobby growled hoarsely, scratching and kicking with all his might. But his grogginess, coupled with my uncanny strength, made his endeavors fruitless. In response, I cranked my death grip even harder. Exhilaration filled my body. My eyes grew large, and my grin quickly widened. The veins in my forearms popped. I felt more than saw his life blood leaving him. In stark contrast, I was more alive than ever.

Killing Bobby was better than sex could ever be.

"Don't feel bad," I teased him. "You were never going to win. At least you're going to have a nice death erection. Larger than life itself!"

His grunting lessened, and Bobby's mouth opened, making him look like a dying fish. "Big man, big muscles," I taunted as Bobby suffered through his last few seconds of consciousness. "Not big enough, I'm afraid... Bye-bye, *boyfriend*," I whispered.

Suddenly, he was completely lifeless and limp in my arms, except for the aforementioned member. When I released my hold, I sat there for a few seconds, cradling Bobby's body against mine as it cooled. Staring at my gloved hands, I looked down at him with amazement. Adrenaline surged through me, and I started cackling uncontrollably like a cheesy cartoon villain.

I'd *actually* done it.

Once the euphoria faded, I realized there was work to be done. So, I enacted the next part of my sinister plan. Retrieving a full, squeaky-clean bottle of NyQuil from my purse, I opened it and dumped its entire contents down the dead man's hatch. Carefully placing the bottle in his hand, I made sure to press his fingers against it, covering the container with his prints.

Surely, the autopsy would reveal a lethal dose of doxylamine succinate in his system. Poor wretched Bobby Downing, taking his own life at such a young age. It was too bad he couldn't cope with losing his position on the team.

Next came the important task of thoroughly cleaning his forehead, his entire face, and his groin - everywhere my mouth had touched. With the help of some washcloths and bar soap, I did just that. I couldn't possibly leave behind any pesky DNA.

Lastly, just in case anyone had overheard Bobby address me as Heather, I planted the seed that perhaps he was mistaken. According to my not-so-real driver's license, the one I'd wiped clean and placed in my purse with my black gloves before I'd arrived, I was never even here. Instead, it seemed that Martha Sullivan from Murrells Inlet, South Carolina was the last person to see him alive.

How unfortunate that she dropped her ID in the hallway on her way out of the hotel before Bobby's self-inflicted demise.

My cleanup was complete. Better judgment kept me from sprinting towards the hotel door. I sat there in the darkness, waiting as other party guests returned to their rooms, hooting and hollering, equally drunken messes. A splendid time was had by all. Well, *almost* all. One hour passed, then two, then three.

Finally, two-fifteen came and went. All was quiet in the hallway outside room 606. Creeping up to the door, I paused to acknowledge one last elevator bell. For five more minutes, I waited behind the barrier with bated breath before making my grand escape. Turning right around the corner and racing towards the stairwell, I rapidly descended six flights of stairs. Chuckling, I recognized another positive of running track for all those years – my efforts caused me nary a labored breath.

Discreetly, I slipped out of the stairwell and turned left, exiting the premises through a side door. Cautiously pressing it closed, I ensured it wouldn't bang and draw attention. I skirted the perimeter and crossed the lot as inconspicuously as I could, remaining vigilant for unexpected strangers. None came.

Things had gone according to plan. There were no positive identifications and no one who knew who I was in the first place, save my prey. As I located my car and slipped inside, the rush of the Atlantic Ocean waves greeted me. Smiling, I twisted the key in the ignition and fled, leaving Bobby behind me once and for all.

I *could have* and *should have* stopped there. Bobby's death might have been the last by my hands, but the experience caused a new compulsion to swell inside of me. A purpose. Heather Berard would do more than survive. She would have vengeance for every abused woman. It became my duty to eradicate men like Stan.

Every now and again, I encounter awful, sick men who require elimination before further harm can be done to the human race.

Take Bryan Pettis, the attendant at the gas station two blocks from my apartment who beat and abandoned his pregnant wife. When I was twenty-four, I removed him from the equation. They never found the presumed perpetrator, Martha Rodriguez from Bend, Oregon. She made sure his wife would never again suffer his brutality.

When I was thirty, I eliminated Randy Joyner because he kidnapped a little girl. Again, no sign of the main suspect, Martha Glynn from Wheeling, West Virginia, was ever found.

Then, five years later, I took care of my neighborhood Wing Zone driver, Corey Grich. One of my co-workers informed me he was stealing money from his boss and using it to buy hookers for self-gratifi-cation. Of course, he was married with two kids at the time.

That might seem less egregious to some, but I know the patterns. First, it's hookers, then it's an actual mistress. Then, he comes home and slaps his wife around for even insinuating he'd cheated on her. Fucking hypocrite. I saw Stan's dirty work too many times to look the other way.

On that particular occasion, Corey almost got away. He actually slipped out of my death grip and swung at me, but I was prepared with Plan B: a shot to the balls and a can of pepper spray. He was easy pickings after that. Martha Rogers from Gainesville, Georgia allegedly did the honors. No leads ever led to her arrest.

All the other times were the same, though. I used my feminine wiles to make them think with the wrong head. Once they became nice and hard, I lured them into a compromising position. Then, like a snake, I unleashed my thick, python arms and squeezed their waists with my legs. My massive thighs were strong enough that they could crush a watermelon.

Afterwards, I poured the sleep medicine down their throats to make it appear as though their deaths were either accidental overdoses or tragic suicides.

I became a pro at getting away with murder if I do say so myself. There was no easily detectable pattern to my kills. I was the perfect assassin. No one would suspect my involvement if they saw me in pass-ing. For the past twenty years, I've just been Heather the accountant.

Then came Zach Snow, the mall security guard. He was the man whom I allowed into my life, the one I chose to marry at age thirty-sev-en. By then, the time was right for me to develop an aura of stability, to keep up appearances. Also, my biological clock was ticking. I realized I wanted to be a mother, to actually *see* my child grow up, a luxury Irene was not given. I had to act swiftly.

Much like my male "friends" who came before him, Zach serves a purpose. He knows almost everything about me, except for my occasional dalliances with Bryce Palmieri. It's easier this way. For the most part, he's aware of what happened between my mother and Stan. He thinks they killed each other, and he knows I legally changed my name at a young age to escape their legacy.

Together, we have a son named Mikey. Well, *I* do. What can I say? Zach is a great father figure, but he's too vanilla in the bedroom. That's why I still need Bryce and his carnal desires.

I will admit, though, there are fleeting moments when I'm in the throes of rough sex with my side piece that make me want to end him right then and there. Most recently, his new flavor of the week was out of town. So badly, I yearned to squeeze the love he has for that cunt, Erin, out of his body.

Forget *love*. Bryce is blinded by lust. He doesn't see her for what she truly is. She's going to use him, leave him, and break his heart. I almost feel a moral obligation to end his sorry existence before she does. It would be a mercy killing.

However, I haven't had the nerve to follow through thus far. I keep seeing eight-year-old Mikey just when I'm about to do the deed. Each time, I remember the pain of losing my own parents at the same tender age, through no fault of my own. I can't bear to take Mikey's actual father from him in the same manner. At least, not yet.

Then again, what better way to teach a young child about mortality and loss. After all, I learned those same hard lessons. I suppose it's the circle of death, isn't it?

Either way, it's hard to get away with murder without my trusty gloves and my other tools of the trade. That puts a damper on the whole thing. Maybe next time I'll do the deed.

It would be fun to once again "unalive" someone immediately after an orgasm. Pleasure and pain go hand-in-hand. You've heard of the seven-year itch? Well, it's been eight since I last "unalived" someone. Soon, I'll have to scratch it - one way or another.

I do know this: If and when the opportunity presents itself, they'd better look for Martha Allen from Gallup, New Mexico. I hear she might be cosplaying as Peaks Allure.

Either way, guns don't kill people. I do.

Episode Five: Summer's Coming

1) Mister Friday Night

"So, how do you like Ann Arbor in December?"

Mitch Irvine, Palmieri's CEO, utters those fateful words when he summons Bryce Palmieri to his office first thing Wednesday morning.

"It's cold in Ann Arbor this time of year," Bryce jests, knowing he has no chance in hell of dissuading his boss. With sixteen years of tenure as regional sales manager, Bryce has been to the well too many times. Once Mitch gets an idea in his head, no one can convince him otherwise, not even the company's namesake.

"Fuck the cold," Mitch retorts. "Wear a jacket. It's a college town. They just won the national championship. What do I always say?"

With a dry smirk, Bryce rolls his eyes and recites Mitch's edict: "Strike while the iron is hot."

"Exactly," the slick-haired, Brooks Brothers-attired CEO replies. "There may be snow on the ground, but there's money in the air."

Bryce peers out of Mitch's office window to the bustling streets in the distance and stifles a sigh. Years of impromptu business trips have rendered him weary and numb. It's par for the course, though, so he states the obvious.

"We've never looked into Midwest expansion. I'm still trying to get Florida up and running."

With his typical shit-eating grin, Mitch hands Bryce a printed copy of an email. "Way ahead of you," he responds. "I spoke with Garfunkel's sales rep, Summer Bailey, last night. They own Packwood Mall. A spot just opened up where the old CPK was. Prime real estate for a burgeoning Italian restaurant chain, don't you think?"

Scoffing, Bryce skims the email and asks, "Do you ever sleep?"

"Not a lick," Mitch replies as his desk phone rings. The CEO holds up a finger and quickly answers. "This is Mitch...." There's a brief pause as someone speaks on the other end. "I'll call him back..." The receiver nestles into its cradle with an abrupt click.

Bryce chimes in, "I'm going to need a day or two to put together a—" but he's cut off before the words can leave his lips. Resigned, he watches in despair as the excited, wide-eyed Mitch detaches his laptop from its docking station and spins it around, revealing a ready-made PowerPoint presentation.

"You *really* didn't sleep last night," Bryce notes. "So, what do you need me for? Seems like you've got it handled."

Folding his hands, Mitch leans back in his chair and deadpans. "Monster Energy, my man. But seriously, I need you to close the deal, just like you've done countless times before. I told Summer you were coming Monday."

Bryce's gaze returns to the window as he rises from his chair across from Mitch's desk. The building's soundproofing negates the rush of wind whipping through Northern Virginia, but the flurries and swaying bare branches of the parking lot's trees tell no lies.

"Looks like winter's coming here instead," he jokes, dramatically stretching his back. Then, he shakes his head. "When am I flying out?"

"Sunday afternoon," Mitch advises. "Oh, and I'll email you all of this."

Bryce softly nods, leveling a cool stare on his boss. "Good. I have plans Friday night."

Curious, Mitch raises his eyebrows. "Heh. Hot date, huh?" he asks.

The image of a certain redheaded vixen forms in Bryce's mind, and his expression slowly morphs into a wry smile. Despite the bitter season's imminent arrival, a warm sensation washes over him. Still, he doesn't let on how right Mitch is.

"Something like that," he replies.

As Bryce leaves Mitch's office and heads out to his car, he can't help but mutter to himself, "Your definition of *regional* is pretty broad, pal."

Bryce sinks onto the couch and fires up his laptop. He's set to work remotely for the rest of the week. At the very least, it would seem the boss has gleefully done the majority of the preparation for his Michigan venture. That means less minutia for him. So, Bryce sets up his out-of-office reply and confirms his meetings for the following week. Then, he eases into another kind of project he has planned for the next two days.

The Winged Eagle condominium complex is eerily quiet for a Friday night during the holiday season. The year is nearing its conclusion, yet Bryce has started a new chapter. All stories need a solid beginning, and his tale is as captivating as it gets.

Needing a break from his business ventures, and a way to relieve stress, Bryce has cultivated a writing hobby for the last three years. Unfortunately, by the time he realized his new pastime had only magnified his anxiety, he was already hooked. Eight months ago, he self-published his debut thriller, *Blacksburg Murders*, under the pseudonym Bryce Mayfield. Now, it's time to start writing again.

He stares a hole through his laptop, and his mind begins to wander. Finally, it fixates on Heather's most recent visit. She has been a riddle wrapped in an enigma for the better part of twenty years. Try as he might to understand her ways, her actions still leave Bryce conflicted. Something changed when she was last here.

For two decades, they've maintained a mutually beneficial sexual relationship. During that time, Heather's marriage to Zach has meant little to Bryce. After all, he isn't the one cheating. He's single. She's had everything to lose, yet in an effort to satisfy her needs, she keeps coming back, choosing to engage in all kinds of roleplay while keeping her husband in the dark.

It's been an ideal situation. Bryce has retained the best of both worlds: pussy and tits on a regular basis without the trappings of an actual relationship. In turn, Heather has maintained her committed relationship and satisfied her carnal desires.

Thus, Bryce still questions her recent motives and objections. His gut tells him something is amiss.

Heather knows he and Erin are also sexual partners. This isn't the first time he's had other casual companions. Like him, Erin has her cake and eats it, too. Heather's reaction to the news was strange. When she learned that Erin had ghosted him after their unusual evening in Orlando, she became enraged.

Her reaction makes no sense. What it does make is a compelling plotline.

Shifting gears, he sets his fingers to the keys, ready to clear the chaos in his brain. He forges ahead with the opening sequence of his sequel, *How To Die In Roanoke*:

***

From the moment she regained consciousness, Taylor Morrow knew she was lucky to be alive. Her last clear memory was of consuming an alcoholic beverage in the presence of unsavory characters. She felt an uncomfortable sensation as she stumbled groggily into the bathroom. At first, it wasn't painful but awkward.

Taylor sat down on the toilet and leaned forward, trying to establish her current situation. The glass doors on the shower to her right were beaded with traces of water. The air was still humid from the steam. Absently, she concluded it had recently been used. She rolled up a handful of toilet paper and gently wiped herself, finding a trickle of blood on the white sheets.

Taylor rose from the toilet seat. She closed her eyes and did her best to replay the evening's events. Like a slot machine at a casino, a vision of her sitting at the bar at the Atlas nightclub suddenly sprang into her mind. She remembered taking that glorious shot of Fireball and looking down at her emerald Mac Duggal evening gown. Only darkness followed. Taylor struggled to fill the spaces in between.

As she stood there, the pain she thought would not come suddenly struck her with a vengeance. She doubled over, and her features contorted with agony. She grazed the shower bar, knocking the panes together. Then, she pivoted and placed her hands on the elongated vanity for stability.

Don't make a sound, she warned herself. Attempting to remain quiet, she quickly bit her lip. *Just get dressed and run. Get out of here.*

With no frame of reference to draw from and no earthly way of knowing the origin of her physical anguish, Taylor counted to ten, taking deep breaths in between each number. She looked in the mirror and saw a tattered young redhead with underwear intact, but breasts barely covered. Readjusting her size 42D bra, she turned to flush the toilet and suddenly stopped. Her left hand hovered over the handle. *No! He'll hear you.*

Instead, she carefully opened the bathroom door and scurried around the floor next to her bed. Bending down, she tried to find her clothes. Her dress was not there.

The digital clock read 5:48 AM.

With sunlight on the horizon, Taylor feverishly searched the room and found her gown lying in a heap on the end table in the opposite corner. The mystery man's white polo shirt and black drawstring shorts rested beside it.

Fearing he might wake at the sound of her layered ruffles crinkling, she snatched his shirt and shorts then grabbed her purse off of the nightstand.

Don't even put them on here. Run!

***

The phone alarm breaks Bryce's rhythm and concentration, imploring him to "rise and shine" at five-thirty in the evening. Hastily, he looks over and uncharacteristically panic.

"Oh, shit!" he bellows. "Dinner!"

Without a moment to spare, he saves his Word document, abandons his computer, and rushes into the bathroom to check his appearance. After a few strokes of his comb and a splash of water on his face, Bryce peers into the mirror.

"Perfection," he confirms with a grin. "Just what the lady in red deserves."

Normally dressed to the nines, Bryce opts for a more casual look tonight. He slips on a red sweater over the top of a t-shirt, then dons his black Swiss Tech jacket. It'll be a nice change of pace. Besides, he figures he and his date won't be clothed for long. At least, not after they arrive at Erin's apartment.

Marching through the condo, he does his usual last check — *wallet, keys, phone, sex appeal.*

"Got'em all," he declares.

Shutting the door behind him, Bryce heads for the flight of stairs two doors down, descends, and exits the building. With the push of a button, he starts his Range Rover and climbs in. A thin, frosty layer on his windshield gradually thaws.

Just as he's about to pull out of his parking space, a thought strikes him. Bryce recalls meeting Erin in person for the first time and formulates a better plan. He wryly smiles as he reaches for his phone. Then, he texts her his Plan B, laughing devilishly.

> *Remember when you were out of town the day I flew to Orlando? It's my turn to do the bait-and-switch. Date Night is at our special place instead, just like that first night we met for real. I'll be waiting… Cum as you are.*

Feeling triumphant, Bryce peels out of the parking lot and drives like a man possessed. Even though the destination is close, he insists on being at Palmieri's well ahead of his date. With ten minutes to spare, he finds a spot in the Ashburn Village parking lot. Knowing he'll receive his customary welcome from the Friday night crew, he swaggers in.

Frank Sinatra's soft crooning drifts from the outdoor speakers as Bryce approaches the front entrance. The music carries over once he's inside, though it is quickly drowned out as Miranda, the new host, and Paulo, the manager, welcome him.

"Bryce!" they exclaim in unison.

Trying in vain to remain stoic, Bryce can't hide his warm delight.

"Hey Paolo. Hey, Miranda," he says. "You made it a whole week with this jabroni."

"Mister Friday Night is back," Paolo announces, arms extended. "With jokes, too." He swiftly rushes over to Bryce and hugs his muscular frame.

"We've got your usual table ready, Sir," the manager advises.

"Thanks, Paolo."

The six-foot-two, dark-haired manager's maroon blazer barely masks his beefy build. "How've you been, man?" he asks as he playfully pats Bryce's back.

"Ah, the usual," Bryce replies, wincing. "Work, work, work."

"Well, you know what they say," Paulo answers. "All work and no play..."

Bryce snickers and offers a perfectly macho yet cryptic response. "Yeah. I might be playing later tonight."

Momentary laughter passes between the two, and Paulo leads Bryce over to his corner seat. Festive garland runs along the restaurant ceiling. Red and green tinsel wraps the large photo of Sinatra, while Dino wears silver. It's the very place where he and Erin first met in person two weeks ago. Situated in the front room, the table overlooks the parking lot.

Bryce stares out into the sea of pavement, cars, and streetlights, expecting to see his favorite redhead arriving with her normal flair and allure. As usual, his thoughts drift, shifting randomly. The holiday decorations trigger a flashback of a Christmas two decades ago.

Vince and Linda Palmieri always loved Orlando. It was only fitting that Bryce, then twenty-four, and his older brother, twenty-six-year-old Shane, bought them an all-expenses paid trip for their father's fiftieth birthday. It was a glorious vacation for the family of four. That was the last Christmas Bryce had with his father.

"Mister Bryce, I presume?"

An unmistakable voice brings his mind back to the present and triggers a shot of adrenaline.

Unable to hide his smile, Bryce turns his head towards the entryway expecting to see his auburn dream. Erin's well-chosen dark green Nmoder Midi Dress is stunning. Her body remains just as he's always known it to be: curvy, self-assured, and immaculate with breasts that introduce themselves well in advance of her arrival. The hair is not hers, though. Her vibrant red strands are as black as a cold winter's night.

Instead of his redheaded vixen, a dark-haired raven, a stark reminder of his most recent encounter with Heather, grins at him. With a face full of fear and ambiguity, Bryce stands and greets his date. He tries in vain to calm his unfounded anxiety.

"You..." he replies, unsure of how to address the situation. He quickly tries to reset and establish a forced smile, but the longer he eyes Erin, the more he sees Heather.

"Miss Erin, you've gone black," he declares.

"Yeah, and I've left my lair for your playground yet again," she teases. "Playing hard to get, tonight, Sir?"

Bryce stares long and hard at the woman he has pined for. He knows he should answer her, but he can't. His breath becomes more labored, and his eyes see red. Though Erin does not resemble Heather, he can't erase the image of the towering Amazon who gets off on causing him both physical and mental anguish.

In a last-ditch effort to regain his composure, Bryce closes his eyes. However, his efforts are futile. Erin reaches in for an earnest hug, and he's unable to escape. Slowly, he recoils, drawing a worried look from his beautiful date who was only pretending to be bothered by his last-minute alterations.

"Bryce!" she exclaims. "What's wrong?"

He gazes at her trying to downplay his panic. Faking his usual confidence, he nods in a feeble attempt to pretend all is well.

"Nice to see you," he deadpans.

Expecting Bryce to be a gentleman, Erin waits for him to pull the chair out for her, but when he makes no effort to do so, her delight turns to disappointment. Instead, she takes off her coat and does the honors herself, sitting down across from him.

"Bryce, is something wrong?" she presses, attempting to decipher his odd behavior.

Bryce doesn't meet her gaze. He tilts his head to the side, an atypical reaction for a normally self-assured man. When he finally speaks, he's almost cold.

"You changed your hair," he offers.

Erin's brow furrows in confusion. "Is *that* what's bothering you?" she asks. Annoyance creeps into her tone.

"Oh, no!" he replies. "I was just... you know, expecting the old Erin." His poor choice of words strikes her like a blow. Before she can object, he adds, "But, this is nice. Sleek and sexy... Like you."

She wants to believe him, but her gut tells her Bryce is being less than genuine. Still, she attempts to heed her father's words. *Choose your battles.*

"You look casual tonight," she responds, attempting to ease the tension. "Cool, relaxed... It's refreshing to see you with your hair down, so to speak."

Smirking, Bryce strokes his short locks. "Thank you, Miss Erin. Still blonde. But yeah, I had to be me tonight."

Still blonde. Had to be me? An all too familiar sense of pain and regret settles into her stomach. His pointed words, rude and misguided, hit their mark, sparking her own unwelcome flashbacks.

Erin's thoughts drift to another man, a young, arrogant Dean insisting he had no problem with her going from a size eight to a size twelve in their four years together. Yet three months later, it was he who broke it off, shattering her heart further when, two weeks later, he changed his Facebook profile photo to show both himself and a petite blonde smiling delightfully at the camera.

Immediately after, Erin's sordid memories of her flight career rapidly resurface. All of the men who only wanted her for her body... All the *upstanding* males who expressed their love for her and showed their true colors just as quickly... Scott, whose unannounced deletion from social media and disappearance from her life remains an unsolved mystery...

Erin swallows, struggling to remain composed. This isn't like Bryce. He's never made her feel this way. Not in all the time she's known him, even going back to their formative teen years.

"We could always play 'Do the curtains match the drapes?'" she suggests, hoping to lighten the mood. Perhaps, the challenge will make him reconsider his attitude.

"We could," he answers, robotically, still refusing to look her in the eye. "It's funny you'd suggest that. I have a friend who has jet-black hair. Spoiler: They do not match. I have a suspicion yours won't, either."

What the fuck? Erin's heart starts to race, and her mind and body begin to seethe. How dare he? Not only hasn't he shown interest in her as a person this evening, but now he's bringing up another woman? On *their* date? The conversation leaves a sour taste in her mouth.

"Well, you sure know how to check for that," she responds. This time, she doesn't bother to hide her frustration. *Two can play at this game.*

Feeling strangely betrayed, Erin looks back at Bryce, noting his distant stare and his slumped body. He's not the man she expected to meet here tonight. Yes, the two of them share a mutual desire for shallow, physical pleasures. That much they'd always agreed on. But, until now, she had never thought he was a shallow human being. Bryce had always given her his undivided attention, in more ways than one. This doesn't make sense.

So what if I dyed my hair? I'm still me, she thinks. *Why does it matter? Good Lord, it's happening all over again.* Tears build behind her eyes as she battles with her anger and embarrassment. *What did I expect, though? Our relationship is based on me sending you nude photos over social media. Shame on me for believing anything more would come of this.*

A young woman stops beside their table, staring at them expectantly.

"Hi, welcome to Palmieri's, home of the Amore Special!" their waitress,

Charlotte, chimes in, interrupting the ruinous moment. Her bright smile stands at odds with the disaster unfolding before her. "Can I get you both something to drink?"

"Oh," Bryce responds, sitting up straighter in his chair. "Yes, I'll have a scotch sour."

"Great, and for you?" Charlotte asks Erin.

Unsure of her next move, Erin pauses and studies the menu. Then, she smiles as she notices a special item on the drink card.

"May I have that strawberry martini?" she politely requests.

"Of course, and do we need a minute to decide on appetizers or entrees?"

"I'm afraid so," Erin promptly answers.

"No problem. I'll get those drinks started for you." Charlotte politely nods and walks away, leaving them alone once more.

Suddenly snapping out of his funk, Bryce clears his throat and attempts to assuage Erin with some familiar banter.

"You can always defer to your favorite," he offers. "Just like we did in Orlando."

Erin gawks at Bryce, who seems completely unaware of the awkwardness he's caused. Oblivious, he catches the eye of another male server, and waves to him. She shakes her head, dumbfounded.

"Hey, Joe," Bryce says. "How about those Nats?"

"How about them?" Joe responds, lightheartedly. "They suck, and they're gonna suck again next year."

"Yeah, I know. Still fun to watch."

If this is how the night's going to go, I'm officially done.

Taking advantage of this momentary distraction, Erin discreetly texts her best friend, Stephanie.

Call me NOW! Op: Exit Strategy

She places her phone face down discreetly on the table before her and studies the menu once more.

Seemingly refocused, Bryce finally turns back to Erin.

"Sorry," he says. "It's been a rough week. I have to go to Michigan on Sunday."

Erin feigns interest and beams. "Oh? What's in Michigan?"

"Uh, presumably another Palmieri's location."

Erin waits patiently as he talks about his travel plans and the potential for Midwest expansion. An awkward silence settles over them before she finally receives Stephanie's call.

"Sorry, I have to take this," Erin explains before answering, lifting the phone to her ear and turning away slightly. "Hello?" She pauses, pretending to listen. Faking shock and horror, she rearranges her expression. "Oh my God! Oh shit! Okay, stay calm. I'll... I'll be right there!"

Quickly, Erin ends the call and stuffs her phone back into her purse. She rises to stand, acting remorseful for cutting their date short.

"I'm so sorry, Bryce," she tells him. "That was my friend. They just took her mom to the hospital. I have to go!"

"Oh no!" he dutifully responds. Giving Erin his undivided attention, he mirrors her sentiment. "Yes, definitely go. Priorities. Listen, sorry, I've been a little distracted. Next time, I'll be more present. But yeah, let me know how she is. I hope everything's okay."

Erin nods and pushes her chair in. Feverishly throwing her coat and purse over her shoulder, she looks at Bryce, keeping a straight face. "I'll let you know."

Tentatively, Bryce reaches for a hug, but then he stops short, finally catching on. He tries once more, but Erin pats his cheek instead.

"Bye!" she says, exiting on swift feet. She doesn't look back until she's out the door.

Watching his date walk briskly out of the restaurant jars Bryce's mind. Embarrassment floods him as he realizes his foolish behavior was unacceptable. Instead of rejoicing in his bait-and-switch like he'd expected to, he's too busy feeling sorry for himself.

Oh my God, I can't believe I did that.

"Damn," he softly mutters when Charlotte returns with two drinks, unaware of Erin's departure.

"Okay, strawberry martini and a scotch sour," she declares, placing the drinks down. "Do we know what we're having for entrees?"

Solemnly, Bryce gazes out into the parking lot to where his date's car should be. Erin is gone like the wind. His sorrow intensifies.

"She had an emergency," he says, turning back towards Charlotte with puppy-dog eyes. He gestures to Erin's empty seat. "It's just me tonight. No Amore Special, literally or figuratively."

The server pauses, confused, unaware of the double meaning behind her customer's remarks.

"Okay... Uh, we have other specials?" she suggests. "Can I get you something else?"

Bryce rubs his temples and shifts into his public persona. "Um, chicken marsala, please," he requests, attempting to save face. "It's the next best thing."

As Charlotte leaves, Bryce unconsciously strokes his hair once again. With each moment that passes, the gravity of his mistakes become more apparent.

"The hair," he whispers. "She's not Heather... Ugh, I'm so stupid."

Despite his meal, his affliction with dark hair proves to be his undoing. The rest of his evening is rendered a well-deserved, bittersweet dinner for one.

2) The Total Package

Twelve hours after their disastrous dinner, Erin is still seeing red. Thus, it's only fitting she finds herself at the nearby Red Theory Fitness bright and early on Saturday morning, ready to burn some calories.

The unmistakable aroma of sweat greets her when she enters the building. She scans her new laminated membership card. The toned girl at the front desk pays her no mind. Not even Erin's classic neon green sports bra and bicycle shorts draw the other woman away from her phone as she scrolls through TikTok.

Erin walks towards one of the many treadmills lined up in the center of the cavernous gym, listening to the audible clinking and clanking of weights. Her muscles tense in anticipation. All she wants to do is run away from last night's awkwardness. Thankfully, there are no wide-eyed men present. Because of her assets, Erin has encountered many a muscle-bound meathead diverting their eyes. They're always too busy looking down at her well-endowed chest to remember their manners. It's made previous gym experiences awkward.

On this day, the only members present are herself, an elderly couple riding the stationary bikes behind her, and a determined, dark-haired female twenty feet in front of her, bench pressing two-hundred pounds.

Intrigued, Erin places her water bottle down in the treadmill's cup holder and watches the stranger. The compelling dark angel pumps the bar up and down with ease, no spotter in sight. The mystery weightlifter must be here alone. Nary a grunt escapes the Amazon's body, only a few labored breaths.

Impressed and captivated by the sheer strength of the woman, Erin stands on the treadmill and delays her workout. She eyes the stranger with wonderment, surprised to find herself thinking, *God, if I weren't straight, I'd want her to ravage me, right there on that bench.*

Finally stepping off, an enthralled Erin slowly approaches her.

The Amazon's muscles ripple, as she guides the bar back onto the rack and pauses. Her skin barely glistens through her black tank top and shorts. With eyes full of conviction, the tall woman slides down the bench and stands, then adds more weight.

Erin uses this opportunity to start a conversation as the stranger slides the plates onto the bar. "Do you need a spotter?" she asks.

Glaring back, the woman tightens her gloves and declines. "No, I'm good."

She then furrows her brow and playfully chuckles upon noticing Erin's bright attire. "Are you guiding planes down the runway with that outfit?" she jests.

"Haha, no," Erin snickers. "It's funny. I *used* to be a flight attendant, but this is just an old sports bra. I wore it all the time when I went hiking."

The powerful woman nods and secures the plates in place with a pin. "Ah, bright colors so they can find you if something happens, right?"

"Exactly!"

The woman flexes her arms as she studies Erin. She reaches back to adjust her hair tie, and her bulging biceps pop, seeming to glow underneath the fluorescent lighting. Barely able to stifle her gasp, Erin surveys the stranger's body.

Brains, muscles, and breasts... Jesus Christ! The total package!

"I think these might be the only body parts where I have you beat," Erin jokes, pointing to her ample breasts.

The Amazon moves to the other side of the bar, adding an extra twenty pounds. She looks back at her assets and shrugs in concession before waving her hand in front of her own tits. "True, but I've never had any complaints."

"I'd be shocked if you had." Erin shakes her head at the notion. "Well, I'll let you get back to hanging and banging.' She winks. "I'm Erin, by the way." She offers a small wave in greeting.

As though Erin has flipped a light switch, something in the woman's demeanor changes. The stranger stops abruptly and narrows her eyes. Keeping her eyes fixed on Erin, she approaches, stone-faced. Her lips form a tight smile, and she extends her gloved, chalk-caked palm.

"Nice to meet you. I'm..." She hesitates for only a second. "Martha."

A dusty white layer clouds the air as they shake hands.

"I like your hair," Martha offers as she grazes Erin's wrist. Her touch lingers there for a few seconds. Pulling away, she decides to end her workout instead.

"Well, time for me to shower. Enjoy your workout... Erin." She smirks.

Erin gasps as the perfectly proportionate Martha turns and walks away, Once the woman is out of sight, she looks down at her whitened hand. Brushing the chalk residue against her thigh, she hurries back to the treadmill, finds her phone, and sends Stephaniea text.

Steph! Wake up. I think I just had my first lady boner for an actual lady in twenty years. LOL

Erin's mind lingers on Martha for a while as she runs like the proverbial hamster. After a time, her thoughts turn towards the man who wouldn't give her the proper attention the night before. Gradually, her irritation with Bryce subsides. She drops the treadmill's speed and lifts her arms above her head, catching her breath.

That wasn't like Bryce. Something must have happened. Maybe I overreacted... I've been burned before, but that's not his fault. I'll text him later and find out what's up. Give him another chance.

A sense of accomplishment settles over Erin as she steps off of the machine. She checks the display and grins. She'd powerwalked for thirty minutes.

"A hundred and sixty calories burned?" she whispers. "Yeah, I'll take it."

More gym members saunter into Red Theory Fitness as the sun gradually brightens in the December sky. Grabbing a towel out of her bag, she wipes the sweat from her forehead, opting to shower at home. Always wary of her appearance in short, tight clothing, Erin quickly puts on her long-sleeve shirt, gathers her belongings, and exits before the inevitable ogling ensues.

As she climbs back into her car, a wave of devious inspiration strikes. Like a mischievous teenager, Erin removes her overshirt, grabs her phone, and smoothes back the sides of her sweaty, damp hair.

"Oh, how am I going to do this with one hand?" she wonders aloud, glancing around her car. "Can I prop my phone up on my steering wheel?"

Sure enough, she can. Erin leans her cell against the top of the wheel, angling it so it rests on top of the center airbag. "Stay..." she commands.

She waits for another passerby to enter the gym then jerks her head left and right, scanning her surroundings. No one is watching, and her android remains stationary. With one calming exhale, Erin lifts her bright-green-clad chest, and gingerly presses the record button. She stares directly into the lens and makes one of her classic, suggestive videos.

"Hey, Babe! I just came from the gym. Well, I didn't *cum* at the gym, per se, but I thought of a way to make *you* cum while I was there. You see, I found this bright green sports bra. Perhaps it could brighten *your* day."

She places her hands underneath the spandex hugging her sternum, preparing for her big reveal.

"I can go for another hour, at least. What do you say? Would you like to *cum* down here and workout with me? I'd love to see how much those *big muscles* can bench. Maybe I can be your *spotter*, hmmm? Would you like me to watch you lift?"

Then, with one fell swoop, Erin raises her bra to free her large tits.

"Or would you like to lift *these* heavy bags instead?" She winks. "You know, it's a good thing you didn't see me running naked on the treadmill earlier. You definitely would've had to wipe down your equipment after using it."

Erin pauses to laugh, making sure her breasts bounce mightily before concluding her naughty video.

"So, what do you say? Would you like a *personal* training session with me?" she asks furtively. "You don't need to buy the deluxe package, although I'm sure by now *your* package is quite large. Oh, did I tell you I specialize in *lower* body exercise? That's right, Big Boy. Cum to *my* gym!"

Erin stops recording and immediately pumps her fist in triumph. As she does, her cell falls off the steering wheel and lands on the car floor, interrupting her. "Fudge!" she complains.

Quickly, she unlocks the door, but as she's about to step out and retrieve her phone, Erin remembers two major issues.

"Oh, shit. Boobs!"

Swiftly pulling down her top, she snatches her cell. Anxiety ripples through her body. She jumps back into the driver's seat and slams her door shut behind her. Her heart races feverishly as she leans her forehead against her steering wheel in dismay.

"Tha twas a close one. I'll post the teaser pic when I get home," Erin tells herself.

But as she starts her car, Erin catches an image in her peripheral vision. Gasping, she turns left and finds none other than her new dark-haired, physically gifted acquaintance staring back, giggling like a schoolgirl. Her heart sinks like an anchor in ocean waters.

Oh, Martha! Please tell me you didn't see... Fuck!

Through the raised side windows of both vehicles, Martha mouths "Nice Rack" to her before offering a casual two-finger salute.

Mortified, Erin presses her hands against the back of her head and closes her eyes, hoping against hope she dreamed this whole thing. She begs to awaken somewhere else, anywhere else. Alas, when she opens her eyes, Erin is still at Red Theory Fitness. More people come and go as day breaks. Martha has since driven away, having seen more than she expected.

Defeated, Erin can only drive home as well. Upon arriving at her apartment, she sits in her car and contemplates her misdeeds. There's nothing she can do about her mishap now, so she laughs and rests her head against her seat.

"Well, at least I know Ican still bag both genders with my sinful ways."

3) Magic Wand

Normally, Bryce would be aware of his surroundings, especially in a strange city and a new airport terminal. However, this time he's distracted. The errors of his ways have been eating at him since Friday night, and Erin's check-in message the next day left him with an additional stinging reminder of his embarrassing behavior.

Even now, as he deplanes and walks through Detroit Wayne International's vast concourse, all he can do is lament the vast opportunity he wasted.

An automated announcement confirms the time: five in the afternoon, reminding passengers that Detroit is in the Eastern Time Zone.

"No shit, Sherlock," he quietly states as he proceeds down the hall, following signs and arrows and walking down escalators.

Like he has so many times before, Bryce goes through the motions, making his way to baggage claim. He stops at carousel four, but the conveyor belt has not yet begun deploying the passengers' checked luggage. His thoughts drift to Erin as he waits for his baggage to arrive.

Okay, just be calm, he thinks. *Say you're sorry. She'll be cool and sexy again. You can salvage this.*

Anxious, Bryce pulls out his phone and finds Erin's PG-rated personal Instagram profile at the top of his page. He clicks on messages, intending to reach out, but instead, he fixates on their last piece of conversation.

> *Hey Mister Bryce! Just checking you see how you're doing. I had the strangest dinner date on Friday night. See, I met this guy who looked like you and spoke like you. He wasn't you, though. He was a distracted, self-absorbed dickhead – totally not the Bryce I know. Please let me know if you're alright. I truly hope so.*

The carousel starts to turn, and the bags begin to descend. Overcoming his fears, Bryce takes a deep breath and finally responds:

> *Hey, Miss Erin. I'm sorry you had to deal with that prick on Friday. I've met him a few times myself. Not the nicest guy or the most logical. I promise you when I get back from Detroit, we'll meet up for real. I'll make sure that other guy stays home. I truly hope you're well!*

As his blue suitcase slowly inches towards him, Bryce briefly shuts his eyes and whispers to himself, "Please give me one more chance." When he opens them again, he snatches his bag and leaves the carousel, descending another series of escalators and heading towards the exit.

The automatic doors whoosh open, carrying with them a glaring chill. Though night has arrived, the falling snow gives the sky a noticeably white hue. Bryce groans as he zips up his winter coat and dons his grey beanie.

"I miss Florida. I miss night swimming," he says to himself, bemoaning the current atmospheric conditions.

As though they are second nature, Bryce walks through his next steps barely batting an eye: shuttle bus, rental counter, show license and confirmation number, tap business card, Bay 43, Kia Sportage, keys on the console, automatic start, set destination on navigation system.

He exits the offsite car rental location and, with the help of the GPS, immediately locates I-94 West, marveling at the ease with which he has found his way.

They knew what they were doing, putting that airport so far outside the city. No crazy traffic.

Handily, Bryce motors through the twenty-minute drive to Ann Arbor. Before he knows it, he's found his way to State Street, the circular road that surrounds Packwood Mall. He locates his final destination, the Paris Garden Inn, standing in the distance like a beacon overlooking the masses. As he drives towards the hotel, he notices the mall entrance, along with a vacated anchor tenant space to his right.

"Six thousand, five hundred feet. Yup. Gotta hand it to you, Mitch. This could be a nice addition. But why here? And why me?" He pulls into the parking lot and stares at the mall through his window. It's remarkably close. "At least we can walk to it from here."

The Mid-Atlantic regional sales manager grabs his bags and wheels them through a set of automatic sliding doors. He expects to see a front desk, but instead, Bryce is taken aback when he enters a casual seating area adjacent to the hotel bar.

The black-vested bartender, whose nametag reads "Michael," spots the lost Bryce and immediately points him in the right direction.

"Check-in is down that hallway to the right," he advises.

Bryce nods and turns in that direction. "Thanks!"

A few minutes later, Bryce obtains his room key, but his mind is still scattered, thinking of other things. He stands in front of the wrong elevator, completely unaware until he hears the "ding." The doors remain closed as he takes a step forward. Confused, he turns, searching for the right lift. Behind him, a blonde woman emerges from the correct elevator, and he nearly crashes into her.

"Ope, sorry!" Bryce exclaims to the shocked lady before entering the elevator she'd just vacated. She gives him a tight-lipped smile and disappears.

Shit, it's happening already, he thinks. *I've been here thirty minutes and I'm already speaking like a Midwesterner.*

He finds his room easily enough, strips, and changes into his usual Spiders t-shirt and grey sweats. The space is nice, but the modern amenities do not sway him. He's been there and done that. Too many hotels. Too many perks.

Disrobing, Bryce lays on the bed, intending to crash. He then thinks better of it and powers on his laptop. He needs to blow off steam. One hour of writing should do it. Instead, he finds himself staring at the screen. The words are hard to come by. Eventually, he eeks out a few paragraphs.

***

The ground floor slowly appeared. At the sound of the bell, Taylor began to sprint, stopping just short of crashing into the trash and recycling receptacles. Pushing off from the wall, she pivoted and ran in the opposite direction, rounding the corner towards the exit as quickly as she could.

The massive, newly renovated atrium was still quiet and mostly empty. A dark-skinned female janitor swept the hallway in the distance. The raggedy-haired front desk clerk listened to music on his Beats headphones. He didn't even lift his head as Taylor dashed out of the automatic doors and into the illuminated parking lot.

"Please be here" she begged, halting and scanning the unloading area.

First, Taylor ran right and stopped short. Then, she surged left, hoping against hope her vehicle was parked somewhere. Sure enough, her eyes bulged as she found her brand-new Kia Sportage far off in the distance. The artificial brightness from the streetlight above lit up the temporary plate like a beacon.

Her stolen shorts began to slip off of her hips, threatening to bare her, as she rushed fifty yards towards her safe haven. Awkwardly, she clutched them, holding them in place, as she dug her key fob out of her purse. Pulling them back up with her left hand, she pressed the unlock button with her right, swung the driver's side door open and dove in. The door slammed with finality as she settled in her seat. Key in ignition, reverse, drive... Freedom!

Taylor didn't need to check her GPS for the directions home. She'd made this trip numerous times before, albeit with less disastrous results. She left the parking lot behind, made a swift left, and drove up the entrance ramp. After a few more twists, she was on I-581 North, then I-81 North, and in the clear.

The clock struck six, and the darkness of nightfall gave way to civil twilight. The misty sky offered the recent college graduate no favors as she barreled up the Blue Ridge Mountains faster than ever. Her Kia blew past nocturnal truckers in excess of eighty miles per hour as daylight slowly crept in. Sunrise morphed the mist into pure fog. Visibility was less than a quarter of a mile, mile, but Taylor had tunnel vision. She saw clearly into her soul as she blazed passed the I-64 junction. A trickle of light opened the overcast skies.

Only then did Taylor's breathing begin to stabilize. No one was coming for her. The realization turned Taylor's fear into hatred. Her hate shifted to anger. Anger called forth repressed memories. The man she'd left behind, sleeping peacefully in that bed, was Darren.

***

Bryce lifts his hands and rubs his temples. There will be no more words tonight. His characters are no longer speaking to him. So, he backs away from his screen and checks the time: seven-forty-five. It's getting late, and he hasn't eaten.

After his trip, he has no desire to even go across the street to the mall food court. Instead, he bites the bullet, throws on a blue sweater, exchanges his sweats for jeans, and saunters back downstairs to the lounge.

Bellying up to the bar on the last stool, Bryce nods at Michael, the bartender, who recognizes him from their earlier brief exchange.

"Hey, you made it," Michael says cheerfully as he places a coaster down in front of Bryce. "What are you having?"

"A little bit of culture shock, I think," Bryce jokingly replies. "I expected to see the front desk at the front entrance."

"Yeah, no!" Michael answers. "At least five times a day, I have to tell people, 'Check in is *that* way.' "

"I bet you get some lost Buckeye fans here at least once a year," notes Bryce as he extends his right arm towards the exit behind him. "Do you tell them check in is about five miles *that* way?"

Michael cackles at Bryce's barb. "Yeah, right! *We don't serve your kind here!...* But, yeah, we like our Wolverines, ya know?"

As if on cue, Bryce looks up at one of the large TVs and finds the Capitals-Blackhawks game in progress.

"Beat those shitheads!" he implores his hometown team. "Oh, uh, sorry... Can I just have a water and a menu?"

"Yeah, no. They *are* a bunch of shitheads," Michael agrees. "Alright, water and menu. Sure thing."

In short order, he brings both. Then, he briefly departs to tend to the other side of the bar.

The lounge area behind Bryce is well-lit but mostly silent, excluding a few hotel guests who are busy typing on laptops and a couple of murmuring patrons. One of those voices percolates and snags Bryce's attention.

"...Summer Bailey. I'm currently out of the office until Tuesday, December 12th. If you require immediate..."

Bryce turns and finds a well-endowed blonde sitting on the couch. Dressed in a navy sweater and tight jeans, the lady in question is not only the one Bryce is supposed to meet with the next morning, but in a twist of fate, she is also the woman whom he nearly collided with at the elevator.

Returning to take his order, Michael asks, "Hey, have you decided?"

Grinning, Bryce nods, "Yeah, I'll do the southwest chicken wrap."

"Good choice," Michael responds. "I'll get that in for you."

When the bartender leaves yet again, Bryce ponders approaching Summer. He recalls the numerous times he has encountered would-be female clients and business associates at a hotel over the years. More often than not, he won them over with one of the four things heal ways carries with him: his wallet, keys, phone, or his sex appeal.

With her golden hair down, her red lipstick prominent, and the absence of a ring on her left hand, Bryce surmises this would be an easy victory. Perhaps this is what Mitch meant when he said to close the deal?

No time like the present. I'll just say hello and be cordial.

Allowing his carnal desires to take the lead, Bryce stands from his stool, adjusts his hair, and stalks over to Summer, who is preoccupied with her phone. The closer he comes, the more the thought of being "cordial" leaves his mind.

"Sorry I almost nailed you," he begins.

Raising her head, Summer's demeanor immediately brightens.

"Hi! Yes, that was you!" she acknowledges, eyeing him. His rugged, toned features must pique her interest because she raises her eyebrows and her voice deepens. "Yeah, you didn't quite *nail* me, but the night is young."

Summer's bright smile is a welcome sight. Her spirited voice and raucous laughter are music to Bryce's ears. As they chat, he barely remembers his reason for being in Ann Arbor is for business, not pleasure.

"Well, that's good to know," he states, casually extending his hand. "I'm Bryce Palmieri."

Summer's delightful grin morphs into a peculiar combination of shock and desire. Despite being two inches shorter than Bryce, the five-foot eight sales rep stands in her high heels to meet him eye-to-eye, fumbling over her words.

"Oh my God! You... Oh my God! *You're* Bryce?"

"Yeah, no, yeah," he sarcastically muses, then chuckles.

"Haha! I'm Summer Bailey!" she answers.

Bryce nods. "Yeah, I kinda heard you from over there. Small world, huh?"

Flustered, Summer stammers and struggles to form a complete sentence.

"Um, wow! Yeah, this...This is quite serendipitous. I'm... not really prepared to talk business right now, although—"

Suave and smooth, Bryce calmly reassures her. "That's fine. We don't have to talk business. From what I understand, Mitch has already spoken with you and this whole thing is something of a formality, anyway."

Summer beams at him, arches her back, and raises her arms to play with her hair. Bryce tries to maintain eye contact; however, Summer's subtle body movements are enough to divert his attention towards her bountiful chest.

"Yeah, we did kind of iron out the details," she confirms. "But there is one thing I need to find out before we go into this meeting tomorrow."

"What's that?"

Summer retrieves her travel purse and enthusiastically searches for an unknown item. "Shoot, I can't find what I need in here." Then, she turns her head back to Bryce and brushes her fingers against his forearm.

"You know what? I think I left it in my room. 316," she says. "Um, I know this is a little informal, but would you mind coming with me for just a moment?"

Melting slightly, Bryce smirks and gazes at Summer.

"It's funny. 316 is my unit number back home," Bryce points out.

"Oh!" she responds, playfully shimmying. "Well, come on up to *your* place then."

The irony is not lost on him. He's played this game before in his younger, cavalier days. He remembers luring women to his room and wooing them just like this.

It's moments like these that rendered Bryce a thirty-eight-year-old divorcee after a brief six-month marriage with Megan Smolinski, the former assistant manager at Palmieri's Manassas location.

"I would love to, but I'm starving," he answers. Looking back, he sees Michael pointing at his stool, having just delivered his meal. "Can you give me about twenty minutes to devour this?"

"Sure. That works," she gleefully says. "Hey, *devour* is such a nice word, isn't it? Like, I can't wait to *devour* that Amore Special here in Michigan. See what I did there?" She winks.

His desire-clouded judgment gets the better of him, and he agrees heartily. "I kind of invented that. It's my special dish."

"So, I've heard. I can't wait to taste it."

Bryce has no suitable reply, so he simply grins, clearly recognizing what lies ahead. He stops and ponders one minute detail. "So, you're staying here. You don't live here?"

"Yeah, no. I live in Downers Grove outside Chicago," Summer answers. With more than a hint of suggestive wordplay, she coos, "I *came* here especially for *you*."

"Ah," he replies, retreating to his bar stool. "Alright. I'll see you soon."

"Yup. 316," Summer reminds him as she grabs her purse. "Nice to meet you, by the way."

"Same here."

With Summer gone, Bryce suddenly begins to question himself as he stares at his southwest chicken wrap. His unsuccessful dinner date is still fresh in his mind. Unnerved, Bryce tries desperately to convince himself Summer is not playing one of his old sex games, even though part of him knows better.

"Not everyone is like you, or the way you used to be," he whispers. "Not everyone *thinks* like you. She's talking about food, not sex... But why does she need to see me now?"

Having consumed his dinner and paid his check, Bryce returns to the elevator where he and Summer accidentally met earlier that night. Pensively, he waits for the doors to open. This time, he's facing the right way. Standing aside, he lets several other guests exit.

On his way up to the third floor, Bryce laughs to himself. *This is proof that God has a sense of humor. How the tables have turned.*

Upon exiting, Bryce finds the sign that points towards the room in question. He turns left and begins his slow walk, but as he does, he receives another message from his favorite lady.

> Hey, Mister Bryce. I'm glad you're back. I hope my hair color doesn't sway you when I post my newest teaser video. If it's any consolation, the curtains don't match the drapes LOL. I started going to the gym. I hope you're still up for a little physical exercise! For the usual fifty, you'll get to see my complete workout regimen. You know what to do.

Bryce closes his eyes, and a warm sensation washes over him. A smile as large as The Big House forms on his lips. All he can muster is a whispered, satisfying breath.

"Erin..."

The hallway is strangely quiet. Not one voice is heard. Not one TV is audible. As he approaches room 316 with a sense of confidence, Bryce cocks his fist and raises his arm.

However, for some reason, he stops in mid-air, knuckles inches from the beige door. Bryce blinks and listens. Summer is stirring inside, tapping laptop keys. Briefly captivated, he stands there, so close to becoming his old promiscuous self.

Glancing down at his phone once more, he clicks on Instagram and checks his last message recipient.

ErinGillies703

Bryce smirks and nods, knowing full well the significance of the handle. It's not from "RedheadBombs407." This is the real Erin Gillies, messaging the real Bryce Palmieri. It occurs to him then that she'd also messaged him from her main account the other night.

The gravity of his feelings finally sinks in. Slowly, Bryce backs way from Summer's door. He quickly ducks into a nearby corner, which houses a vending machine, and logs into his work email. Then, he finds the last business-related correspondence from Summer and replies:

Hi Summer,

I have an unforeseen personal matter to attend to this evening. I'll be flying back home tomorrow afternoon. Rest assured, we'll have ample time to finalize the paperwork. The mall is a perfect location for young Michiganders to enjoy our Amore Special. It's our signature dish, as you know.

I'm looking forward to our business meeting tomorrow morning.

Best regards,

Bryce

With a newfound sense of satisfaction, he beams earnestly and shrugs. Reaching into his wallet, Bryce pulls out a few dollar bills and feeds the machine. A can of Sprite plummets to the bottom for the taking. He grabs it and walks back towards his room at the opposite end of the hallway.

In the eerily quiet corridor, the faint sound of buzzing catches his attention. Bryce looks down at his phone, thinking it might be an unusual notification, but it's on silent. A burgeoning moaning drifts through the quiet space alongside that familiar purring sound. At that moment, Bryce comes to a remarkable, unmistakable conclusion.

Someone's getting off with a vibrator.

Turning, he sees a door, and marvels at the location of the blissful whirring.

"Room316," he softly decrees.

Curious, Bryce checks to confirm no one is watching, then inches closer to the hotel room. To his astonishment, he hears Summer's voice echoing words of cathartic self-pleasure.

"Oooh, you already ate, huh? Now it's *my* turn! Oh, Bryce. I want that Amore Special! Ohhh! It's such a big serving, but I've got a *big* appetite! Ohhh!"

Her moans grow louder the closer she comes to that undeniable ecstasy. While Summer's Magic Wand gives her pussy pleasure, Bryce feels a unique sense of accomplishment knowing he's making her orgasm without even laying a finger on her.

The sounds of crinkling sheets tell him Summer's writhing becomes more intense. At that moment, one thought becomes crystal clear.

At least I know the mere thought of me can still bag a woman.

Suddenly, a nearby door creaks open, rousing Bryce and sending him scurrying away. He quickly resumes walking back down the hall towards his destination. A young man, empty beer can in hand, stumbles into the hallway and immediately calls out.

"Hey! Whassup? You good, man?"

Spinning to his right, Bryce eyes the slurring, unshaven hotel guest and confirms as much.

"I'm good, bro," he answers. Then, he motions backwards with his head and grins. "Summer's cumming."

Oblivious and wasted, the young man responds, "Yeah, it is! National champions again! Woooo!"

Returning to his room, Bryce calmly struts over to his king-sized bed. With renewed fire in his eyes as well as his loins, he kicks off his shoes, removes his sweater, and lays down.

Murmuring ensues as more inebriated guests wander the halls. Muffled voices on the TV next door don't faze him.

Bryce snickers.

"National champions, indeed!"

He clicks on his PayPal app and, with a glimmer in his eyes, sends Erin the requisite fifty dollars.

A few more doors slam, and the voices in the hallway subside. Bryce's phone lights up, indicating the arrival of Erin's promised video missive. He lays there watching his favorite lady wax poetic about her gym escapades in her bright green sports bra. As Erin reveals her massive assets, Bryce unbuckles his belt and unzips his jeans.

Bryce holds his phone in his left hand, admiring his lady in all her glory, with growing intensity, dark hair and all. At her encouragement, he lays back and performs his own kind of magic with his right.

"Oh, wow! Yes, Miss Erin!" he exclaims.

A week's worth of buildup means it doesn't take him long to reach the summit. Joyous as it is for Bryce to cum for Erin in Michigan, suddenly the idea of coming home to her in Virginia is even more satisfying.

Episode Six: A Thousand Oceans

1) It's Just A Name

The darkness is fading, both in Bryce's bedroom and in his wounded heart. After a brief, whirlwind trip to Michigan, it's all become clear. Turning down a lust-filled night with Summer in lieu of returning to Erin revealed his true feelings.

Also apparent is his rigid erection, which wakes him from his slumber.

The undeniable throbbing has Bryce ready for anything as he stirs. Only this time, he finds his morning wood is not the result of relaxation. To his surprise, his comforter has been thrown to the foot of his bed, leaving him exposed.

He is not alone.

Bryce's eyes widen as he finds a curvaceous, silhouetted figure pressing down on his quads, sucking his massive cock for all its worth. Her technique is perfect, making him pulse, bringing him to the brink, then slowing down just long enough to back his impending orgasm off.

It's been years since Bryce has woken up to a blowjob. Never before, though, has he been brought back from a deep sleep so primed to explode.

A shaft of light shines through his blinds as sunrise imminently approaches. Bryce peers down to see hair as black as night and huge tits, swaying with the woman's every movement. His smile grows as her hands playfully massage his balls. She licks his shaft from base to tip.

"Oh, Erin!" he cries out then remembers protocol. "Oh, yes, Miss Erin! Please finish me!"

Still cloaked in shadow, she grins deviously as she obliges. She pumps him simultaneously with her mouth and hands, holding him at her mercy.

Bryce's mind races, torn between wanting to whisper, "How did you get in here?" and letting her work her magic. As the sensation builds, he opts to defer until after he cums. He can't ruin this magical moment. Already, he's mere seconds away from the burst of energy he needs. This time, it isn't purely physical. At long last, he no longer wants just her body. He wants all of her to fill his soul.

"Oh, Miss Erin!" Bryce cries out.

Suddenly, she stops and pulls away. The silhouetted woman looks up at Bryce and licks her lips. With eyes as fiery as Hell, her evil intentions are clear.

In a deep, sultry tenor, she commands, "Try again, boy toy."

Adrenaline shoots through Bryce. He tries to rise, only to be thwarted and held down by her thick, muscular arms. Shocked, scared, and still hard, he watches as the burgeoning light reveals his true partner.

"Heather!" he exclaims.

Fast as lightning, Heather pins Bryce to his bed, resuming her carnal endeavors. He tries in vain to fight her off, but his strength is no match for hers. Likewise, his hammer cannot withstand her oral prowess any longer.

"No! Heather! Please, no!" he growls before pleasure overwhelms him, flattening him back onto his mattress.

Bryce's body begins to shake, practically vibrating with need. His brain says "no," but his cock has already been lured into ecstasy by this devil goddess. He cannot escape. As the muscles in his abdomen tense in anticipation, an innate feeling of terror accompanies his impending orgasm.

"Oh, nooooo!"

One more mighty roar escapes Bryce before his warm, copious seed follows suit. Panic washes over him as Heather pauses to admire her handy work. She uses her thumb to collect the remaining fluid on her lower lip, sucking it clean, as he struggles to catch his breath. Once he is rendered motionless, she crawls on top of him and straddles his chest.

Eye to eye with the defeated, horrified Bryce, she smiles. A reddish hue appears in her pupils as a trickle of cum escapes and dribbles down her chin. Softly cackling, an almost otherworldly Heather leans in, nearly touching Bryce's pale, terrified cheeks.

"I knew you'd choose me over her!" she growls.

Bryce screams and jolts awake, sitting up in his bed. His heart racing a mile a minute, he unconsciously mutters "No," before becoming acutely aware of his surroundings. A soft pinging sound emanates from Bryce's baseboard heating unit. His bedroom is otherwise quiet. His comforter has not been discarded. No one else is present.

Bryce glances down and sees his flaccid, unused member inside dry sweatpants. It's six-twelve on a Tuesday morning, three minutes before his alarm is supposed to go off.

"Fucking nightmare!" he complains, attempting to settle down.

Bryce showers and readies for another day in the trenches at the corporate office. As he is about to exit with his usual four must-have items, he receives a text from Mitch.

> Come see me when you arrive. Big Plans. Big Changes!

Disgusted, he sighs. The last four words he wants to hear are 'big plans, big changes.' Still, he gets in his car and makes that familiar drive. Other than the dulcet, easy-listening tones of Dino and Frank echoing throughout the atrium, his workplace is the typical, sterile office building.

Tentatively, Bryce walks into Mitch's office at eight-thirty to find the CEO deep in thought, buried in his Outlook emails. He stands in front of the uncharacteristically oblivious Mitch, wondering what tricks his boss has up his sleeve this week.

"So, where am I going now? Houston?" Bryce sarcastically asks.

Mitch snaps out of his momentary daze and looks at the sullen regional sales manager.

"Bryce, shut the door, please," he orders.

Worried, Bryce does just that. Then, he strides over to Mitch's leather couch against the wall and promptly sits.

Preemptively, he pleads his case. "Look, I don't know what you heard, but we closed the deal. You have your restaurant in Ann Arbor."

"Well, that's why I wanted to see you," Mitch replies. There's something off about his posture. The typically boisterous CEO is slouched and keeps his arms folded. "Well, one of the reasons, anyway."

Leaning in, Bryce asks, "What did Summer tell you?"

"She told me you were attentive to her needs and you were an absolute pleasure to work with," Mitch answers. "Which leads me to the next little bit of information I need to lay on you."

Bracing his arms on his knees, a curious Bryce waits for his boss to drop the other shoe.

"You've been here, what, twenty-one years?" Mitch continues. "Regional sales manager for sixteen of those? So, I feel like you should hear it from me. I'm sure you've heard the rumor and innuendo behind the scenes."

"I've actually been a little preoccupied with other things," Bryce answers.

Sitting upright, Mitch pauses. "Well, it's time to refocus. I know you have a hard time doing that with your, uh, condition," he points out.

Slightly offended, Bryce stands up straight and tall. "I'm fine, Mitch," he declares with conviction. "Now, what's this big news you have for me?"

Mitch proceeds to deliver his missive. "Well, you know, the stock price has been a shrinking violet for two years now, and it's going to become official as of ten this morning. Moocat is buying us for two billion dollars."

Livid, Bryce jumps up. "You're selling my company?" he blurts out.

"Now, hold on. It's not *yours*," Mitch reminds him. "You own stock, just like I do, just like a gazillion other people do. Your grandfather went public twenty-five years ago because your father wanted nothing to do with the business. He didn't want to see it go down the toilet. You know this."

Unable to meet Mitch's gaze, Bryce glares out of the office window into the sea of pavement, focusing on the cars and trees. Numb and dejected, his thoughts once again wander aimlessly to Erin, Heather, his parents, his future...

"Moocat has a presence all over the continental United States," says Mitch. "They also have their own people coming in. Some higher-ups are going to become expendable. You know how mergers go."

Returning to the present, Bryce turns to his boss, annoyed.

"What does that have to do with me?" His voice shakes.

Mitch leans back in his chair and breathes deeply. "Well, I spoke with Moocat's EVP. The new parent company has an opening in the Midwest. Because of your recent success, they want to transfer you to Chicago."

Flying out of his seat, Bryce stalks over to his CEO. His heart races, pounding a samba in his chest. "And if I don't go?"

Somberly, Mitch lowers his head. "Then you don't go, but you also don't... uh, have a job." The boss' revelation shakes Bryce to his core.

"They have a guy coming in to take your position," Mitch continues. "He wants to move here." Gesticulating with his hands, he finishes his train of thought. "It's kind of a weird little condition of the deal. I had no say in that part."

"Mitch, look at me," Bryce responds, furious. The veins in his neck protrude as he carefully enunciates his next words. "My grandfather started this fucking company. It literally has *my name* on it, and you're saying replacing me after twenty-one years is just a *little condition*?"

Mitch raises his hands, begging Bryce to remain calm. "I... didn't mean it like..." He nervously stammers. "I didn't know how to tell you—"

"So, this little trip to Michigan was just a test?" Bryce wonders. "After all these years, you couldn't be straight with me from jump?"

Silently, Mitch sits in his chair. He bows his head and looks off into the distance. Bryce wants desperately to flip every piece of furniture in the room. Fortunately, for the moment, cooler heads prevail.

It doesn't matter what he says. His fate is sealed. The bitter taste of acceptance settles on his tongue. Still, if Mitch wants to take what's rightfully his, then he can take what they want, as well. Planting his hands on his hips, Bryce confirms his exit strategy.

"Well, I have five hundred and seven shares in this company. Last I checked, they were going for about twenty-five per share. Maybe it's time to divest."

"I'm not telling you to do that," Mitch quickly answers, knowing there are clear-cut rules in place prohibiting insider trading. "I never said that. You can't say I did."

Years of working together soften Bryce's response. "You don't have to say it," he replies. Then, he shakes his head. "Truth be told, I've been a little distracted with my side projects anyway. Maybe it's time to let go. I mean, yeah, it's my name on that wall, but... Maybe it's just a name?"

Gradually, the initial sense of disbelief wears off. He closes his eyes, thinking of his grandfather, the man who decades ago founded Palmieri's restaurant, and his own years of service. "I've given a lot to this company—"

"Nobody's denying that," Mitch interrupts.

"Yeah," Bryce nods. Much to his own surprise, a slight smile forms as he considers his future. For the first time, he actually has options. "I'm forty-four years old. I have a lot of dreams left to fulfill. One of them just moved here from Florida."

"A girl?" Mitch wonders.

"C'mon, man," he guffaws. "I've had more than my share of girls over the years. This is a *woman*. This is…"

Struggling to find the words to properly convey his burgeoning feelings for Erin, Bryce reflects on the past several years.

"What do you do when the one that got away comes back twenty-five years later, and you let her get away again?" he wonders. "No. I can't do that. Not this time."

Mitch, more relaxed now, stands and walks out from behind his desk. He, too, smiles as he saunters up to Bryce, proud and relieved.

"She must be special, huh?" Mitch realizes. "I thought I had it with Jillian. We're always looking for that missing piece, aren't we?"

Bryce extends his arm, content to end his professional relationship with Mitch. His boss, however, is not satisfied with a simple handshake. Instead, he grabs Bryce and reaches around for a well-deserved hug.

"Listen, if this is what you really want to do, well… I want you to be happy," Mitch says.

Patting his boss' shoulders, the former regional sales manager nods and stifles a tear. "I will be."

Then, Bryce Palmieri leaves Mitch's office for the last time and walks down the hall to his own. Still, the gravity of his decision doesn't sink in. He doesn't let it fester, for he has other goals in mind.

Before he can think twice about his drastic decision, Bryce grabs an empty box from a nearby printer and proceeds to gather his personal belongings. Remarkably, they are few and far between. Items in his filing cabinets mean nothing to him. Scouring his office, Bryce sifts through his old family photos, including one of himself at age twelve, with his father, Vince, and grandfather, Eric.

Aside from the photos, the only souvenirs he decides to bring home are a framed ticket stub from Game Three of the 2019 World Series, a Ryan Zimmerman signed baseball, and a pair of tiny plastic hands. The latter item perplexes him.

"Why the fuck do I still have these?" he wonders aloud.

Shrugging it off, Bryce places them in the box with his photos, then proceeds to sit at his desk and begin his official resignation email. He should feel trepidation. However, the respectful, gracious words flow easier than anything he penned when covertly writing his first novel.

He doesn't yearn for any pomp and circumstance for his grand farewell. He's already advised his closest confidant of his decision. He plans to text two of his female colleagues later that day, just to let them know personally. With one last check around the office, Bryce sees nothing but easily expendable office supplies.

"Relaxed. No second thoughts," Bryce observes. "Who would have guessed it?"

One last time, he approaches his desk to check the delay settings on his email. His final words are slated to be delivered at four-fifty-five, right before the end of the day. He hits the send button, then casually shuts down his computer, and leaves.

Smiling and nodding to a few random co-workers, Bryce Palmieri exits the building. Only when he is gone like the wind do his colleagues receive word. Suddenly, the man has departed for good, leaving behind his family legacy.

After all, it's just a name.

2) Crossing The Bridge

Until this very moment, Bryce had never set foot in the Ashburn metro station. Careening through the underground during the midday lunch rush was hardly on his radar. He'd never needed nor wanted to ride through the bowels of the nation's capital. Yet, today has unceremoniously become the first day of the rest of his life, and before he embarks on his new journey, there is something he must do. He feels morally obligated to visit the place where Linda, his mother, drew her last breath.

The exposed beige concrete and Brutalist design motifs of the original subway stations trigger bittersweet memories as he travels to his destination. The minutes tick by, harkening Bryce back to simpler times. His thoughts turn to Eric, his grandfather, who'd innocently passed away in his sleep before the Nationals played their first game in their new home city. Then, they drift to recollections of his family's trip to DC as he arrives at Rosslyn station.

Gradually, the train slows to a stop. Sadness and nostalgia grip him as he disembarks, crosses the platform, and awaits the next monorail. He finds himself no longer mourning only his mother's passing, but each of their losses all over again.

After another short ride, Bryce steps out of the Pentagon station tunnel into the crisp December air. Silently, he circles the iconic building, a looming structure of strength and honor, on foot until he alights upon his final stop, the place where his mother's life ceased. Who knew Linda's plane would land there instead of in Los Angeles on that fateful September 11th?

Before him, the illuminated benches surrounding the memorial are as welcoming as they are harrowing. He briskly passes each in turn until he finds the one piece of molded steel with her name engraved at the end.

Though he'd remained poised at the office, seeing her name suddenly brings Bryce to tears. His regrets and fears poor freely from him as he blinks away the salty water clouding his vision.

"What am I gonna do, Mom?" he asks. "It took me four and a half decades to figure out what's really important. I should be happy I'm not with the company anymore, but... God damnit, I lost her. She came back to me all these years later, and I pushed her away. I was juvenile and foolish. I'm the last one standing in our family, but what do I stand for now?"

Of course, Linda doesn't answer. The silence stretches long between his words and the memorial before him. He draws in a few deep breaths and wipes the tears from his eyes. After a few moments, Bryce blows his mother a kiss and gradually wanders back towards the metro station. Just before he descends into the underground once again, he receives a welcome text message.

> Hey, Mister Bryce. I'm hungry, but I'm not interested in going to a restaurant this time. Let's try my place. 6pm? You choose dinner. I'm up for anything, but you know what I like!

Stunned, Bryce grins and looks up at the cloudy sky. Then, he nods as if to thank his family for one last opportunity. With sheer delight, he types out a response.

> The real Mister Bryce will attend. I'm also up for anything, as you well know, Miss Erin.

As the train carries him back home, Bryce's thoughts are preoccupied with his bombshell. He contemplates what he should bring to their date, having effectively ended his career with Palmieri's. By the time he arrives back at the station, the hopelessness that had settled into his soul has dissipated. He laughs, realizing Erin will be expecting her favorite dish. *How do I pull this off?* Bryce wonders.

Perpetually on time, Bryce pulls into Sterling's Dominion Estates Apartment complex at two minutes to six. Opting for a casual look yet again, Erin's dinner date arrives at unit 104 in a festive red sweater and jeans, carrying a white plastic bag.

Erin's apartment door is ajar, an open invitation if Bryce ever saw one. He casually enters. Inside, his dinner companion awaits, smiling brightly, wearing a blue-patterned blouse and matching khakis. Her smile dissolves into a curious expression when she notices the apparent contents of Bryce's bag.

"Well, Sir... That doesn't appear to be The Amore Special," she says.

"Ah, no. This is the Tanaka Express Special," he reveals as he walks in and places the food down on her coffee table. "Pepper steak and shrimp lo mein. Funny story. I, uh, kind of retired today."

"You what?" Erin blurts, with equal amounts of surprise and delight. The smile returns to her face.

Bryce removes his black Swiss Tech jacket and gently places it over the arm of her couch. "Yeah. So, Palmieri's and Moocat Foods merged and..." His words trail off as he approaches Erin. A peculiar feeling overcomes him.

"Do we hug now and kiss later or do all of the above later?" he cheekily asks.

Without hesitation, Erin reaches for his cheek, pulls him to her, and passionately kisses him on the mouth. When she slowly backs away, she grasps Bryce's hands and brings them teasingly close to her ample breasts.

"Let's eat dinner first," she advises, grinning mightily. "Then, we'll eat *dessert* later."

"Sounds like a plan, Miss Erin."

An insatiable gleam shines in her emerald eyes as the now dark-haired maiden responds with a new rule.

"You know what?" she begins. "Let's not do the whole 'Mister and Miss' thing anymore. Let's cross that bridge already and be real with each other. How does that sound?"

Together, they approach the couch to sit next to each other. Bryce tilts his head and takes a long, slow breath. "I appreciate that... Erin," he softly replies.

Erin calmly nods and squeezes his knee. Changing the subject, she presses, "So, after all this time, all these years of galivanting across the country on a plane, you just up and quit?"

"Sounds familiar, doesn't it?" he wryly counters.

Erin laughs, then calmly notes, "It sure does."

"To be frank, I've been getting a little worn down with all the travel," Bryce continues. "I want to do something I truly believe in. Life's too short, you know?"

Taking a sip of her red wine, Erin sympathizes. "Believe me, I know all too well." She tears open the bag of food and reaches in for her meal. "Do you mind? I'm starving. I didn't eat lunch."

Bryce coolly obliges. "Eat your heart out."

He watches as Erin swiftly takes a few bites of her pepper steak. Bryce calmly takes his lo mein and opens the plastic container as she continues her story.

"Flying around the world a thousand times over was so taxing," Erin notes. "Not to mention all the inappropriate behavior I put up with. This was before I leaned into it with my spicy account, mind you."

"Right," he answers before he begins eating.

"But yeah. I needed to take that job at Dulles." Erin raises her glass. "Who would've thought it would lead me to you?"

Only then does she realize her guest is without a beverage. "Oh! Where are my manners?" She shakes her head. "What are you drinking?"

"No worries. Do you have Cold Snap?" he asks.

Rising from her couch seat, Erin saunters over to the kitchen, hips swaying as she goes. "Yup."

She procures a bottle of Sam Adams' winter seasonal from the fridge. As she carries it over to Bryce, she pauses.

"Oh, shoot. Bottle opener. Sorry," she says.

Bryce casually waves her over and takes the beer. Then, he pops it open with his bare hand. "One of my many talents," he muses.

"Ah, you do have many."

Erin reaches for her wine glass and clinks it against his bottle. "Here's to crossing the bridge," she proposes.

Bryce peers tenderly at Erin, his heart warming rapidly. "This is a real date, then?" he questions.

"As real as it gets," she asserts.

After a few moments of silently consuming their Asian cuisine, Bryce lifts a finger.

"Speaking of real, question..."

"Oh. Real question. Fire away," Erin says.

Bryce quickly swallows his food. "How many men engage in uh, fun time, with your Insta?"

"Well, to be honest, you're the only one left," Erin confirms, giggling light-heartedly.

"Nahhhh!"

"Uh-huh."

Surprised, Bryce tilts his head and dramatically crosses his legs. "So, there were others, but now, not-so-much?"

"Oh, I've had *quite* a few over the years," she notes. "But you..."

When Erin doesn't finish her thought, Bryce offers one of his own. "Not too many old middle school and high school classmates have found you, huh?"

Smiling, Erin chases her feelings with another sip of Pinot. "Do you know how hard it was to try to ignore you on that flight to Greenville two years ago?"

Bryce enthusiastically slams his hand on the arm of the couch "I knew you knew me! I couldn't be that guy and say, 'Hey, I'm Bryce. I had the biggest crush on you in high school. I think you're hot.'"

Erin's eyes are as wide as saucers as she says, "I've heard a *lot* worse in my day. And for the record, I totally would have gone out with you then."

Laughing, Bryce shrugs it off and reflects on his youth. "Oh, yeah. Awkward teenage Bryce. Believe me, I've grown up a lot."

Seizing the moment, Erin seductively arches her back. "Oh, you're not the only one... *Bryce.*"

Bryce deliberately uncrosses his legs and puffs his chest like an old gunfighter about to draw. "You could've had any man you wanted, then and now. I find it hard to believe you don't have any other takers on Insta... *Erin.*"

Carefully placing her wine glass on the coffee table, she lays some truth on him. "Well, you're right, of course. I've had my share of men, but I'll let you in on a little secret: After I met you here, I stopped offering my services to everyone else. All except that one other guy from Florida, and he bailed on me, for reasons I still can't figure out."

"Bailing on you is like preferring not to breathe. I mean, Jesus."

"It is what it is," she answers. "It wasn't a total loss. I found a nice young man to take his place, though. He was all too eager. That was a nice win, I must say."

Holding up his hands, Bryce accepts her revelation. "That's perfectly within the rules, right? I mean, you did your thing and I did mine."

Erin barely gets a mouthful of pepper steak down her throat before chuckling. "Oh, so you had your *own* fun, huh?"

"Yeah, it was fun until it wasn't," Bryce admits. "The woman I saw, she's been an on-again, off-again friend for a while. It's taken me this long to realize it'll never be anything more than sex."

Mischief shines in Erin's eyes, intensified by the glare from her standing lamp. She dares to ask. "So, who's better? Me or her? Be honest!"

"Hmmm..." Bryce pauses and playfully massages his chin. Then, he affirms, "It's close, but... you."

Pleased, Erin playfully shimmies. Bryce notices a sparkle in her eyes, which he assumes is due to the holiday lights shining in from outside. "Well, I wish I could say I'm surprised."

As he takes a large sip, Bryce asks for her own sexual synopsis. "Your turn. Who's better, me or Florida Man?"

Erin leaves no doubt. She nearly spits out the last of her wine, attempting not to laugh. "Oh, no fucking contest! You take the cake."

Bryce smirks and subtly pumps his fist. "Was he good at least?"

Boisterous laughter causes Erin to struggle to string together an adequate answer. "He was, um... young? Happy to be there. No, he wasn't good, but he was nice. Very grateful for the, uh, Erin experience."

"I know I'm grateful for the Erin experience," Bryce says before standing. His gaze lands on the corner of the living room where an acoustic guitar sits, carefully placed upright on a stand. Enthralled, Bryce walks over to the valuable instrument.

"That's a Martin special edition OMJM Katie Anderson signature model," she advises. "Got it at Guitar Center for five grand."

"Ooh, I love Black Swan. Do you play?" Bryce wonders.

"Not a lick," she replies before corralling the instrument and throwing the strap over her shoulders like it's second nature. "Well, maybe a little. Okay, it's one of *my* hidden talents."

Amazed, Bryce sits backdown next to her as she starts tuning up.

"Do you like playing with nice, expensive toys?" he jokes.

Erin casually strums until the sound on the acoustic axe is to her liking. Then, she slowly looks up at him and deliberately gazes at his crotch. In a sultry manner, she answers.

"You tell me."

Not waiting for Bryce to respond, Erin begins playing a chord progression in four-four time. *E-Minor, D, A-Minor, C.* Bryce feels the walls around his heart crumbling with each note.

"How long have you been a guitar hero?"

Without missing a step or a chord, his lady in black replies without even glancing up at her dinner date.

"Twelve years. Needed a hobby. Too many lonely nights on the road... Well, when men weren't lining up waiting to sleep with me, that is."

"You learn something new every day," Bryce muses. "How'd you bring a guitar with you everywhere?"

"Don't laugh," she insists. "I didn't. I brought a ukelele with me. Kept the acoustic at home. Too much baggage for a flight attendant, you know?"

Erin waits until the next bar in the seeming endless loop of chords to begin singing the lyrics. "*The river's alive and the winds are peaceful tonight...*"

"Don't laugh. That's my favorite song," Bryce interrupts.

"*Thoughts of your hair glowing at civil twilight—*"

"Remember when Katie went through her redhead phase?" she asks, pausing her own song. "I was so happy. I was like, 'Ooh, another redhead, just like m—'"

Realizing the falsehood looming at the end of her sentence, Erin abruptly stops playing and looks squarely into Bryce's eyes.

"Shit! I'm not a redhead anymore."

Smiling at the dark angel seated beside him, Bryce leans in, love budding in his heart. Erin's chest heaves recognizing the emotion. He can tell things have changed between them. She, too, feels something more than an insatiable desire to fuck. Only the length of the guitar keeps them apart.

"What made you dye it?" he wonders.

"Just needed a change," she answers, conveniently avoiding the true reason behind her motives. "I've had this blazing red hair for forty-something years. I wanted something different."

With renewed assurance, Bryce smiles brightly. His eyes exude want. His heart possesses an unfamiliar longing to hold and caress her for all eternity. Desperately trying to hold it together, Erin resumes playing and crooning, hoping to lose herself through the majesty of song.

"We can love again, if you can only try."

"Sometimes, change is good," he advises, stifling his craving for meaningful affection. "But tell me this... Erin. Who did you change it for? You?"

Pausing to reflect, Erin considers her answer.

"No," she mutters. "I changed to become someone else."

Concerned, Bryce places his hand on the body of the guitar, stopping her from strumming. "Who?" he inquires.

Erin stops, and her expression seems conflicted, like she's fighting back the urge to explain her true thought process. The silence is heavy as Bryce watches her mind race.

Just say something. Anything, he hopes.

"Someone who didn't fall for you the first time she saw you," she eventually answers.

Bryce's body trembles. His heart pounds harder than it ever has. Finally, his second chance at love has arrived, albeit with an ironic refrain from the dark-haired singer swaying beside him on her couch.

"Meet me in Mystic, if only just to say goodbye."

Bryce lunges at Erin, crushing the guitar between their bodies, and firmly kissing her. Erin quivers from the sensation of his hands on her cheeks. Bryce senses her body tingling and feels the sparks igniting inside her for the first time in decades. Erin rises to meet him, lifts the strap over her shoulders, and tosses it aside without a care for its mint condition.

With a sense of purpose he's never felt before, he grips her arms and wraps them around his body.

Their lips are still entangled in a web of desire, as Erin struggles to find the right words, offering an awkward response. "I may have broken an expensive guitar."

His passion rises along with his cock. Quickly, Bryce assures her otherwise. "This is worth more than that. I promise you."

Upon hearing his declaration, Erin's mind and body spring into overdrive. With the force of a winter storm, she pushes Bryce across the living room into the wall adjacent to her bedroom. Momentarily, he panics, the image of a strong black-haired lady still triggering his intrusive thoughts. That fear quickly dissolves when Erin's fingers reach under his shirt and sweater, grazing his pecs, then shift downward onto his rippled abs.

Bryce's mind recalibrates, knowing full-well Heather's modus operandi is to attack him from behind. He reciprocates Erin's advances by cupping her breast and running his tongue down her neckline. She lets out an enormous sigh, exhaling almost forty-four years' worth of relief and desire. Beaming, Bryce reaches inside the front of her dress and massages her massive tit.

"Oh, Bryce!" she exclaims. "This is how it should have been all along."

"Oh, fuck yeah," he agrees.

Clumsily, Bryce pulls Erin from the wall just enough so that he can spin her around the corner and into her bedroom. They nearly fall in a tangle of limbs, but he reaches out to steady himself on the edge of the closet, managing to maintain their balance. Bryce and Erin kiss passionately as she guides him around the side of the bed. He pauses long enough to flick the bedroom light on.

An unspoken truth is realized as the pair look deeply into each other's eyes. Every other time they've pleasured each other, there was an unusual race against time, both of them needing and wanting each other before the moment could end. This time, as Bryce holds Erin's hands and draws her down onto the bed with him, they understand deep within their souls. *The race is over. This is forever.*

In an uncommon miscue, Erin slips and falls directly onto his fully erect eight inches, prompting a painful groan from Bryce.

"Ahhhh!" Bryce cries out, doubled over in pain.

Horrified, Erin covers her face. "Oh, shit! Oh!"

Bryce peers up at his concerned partner and smiles as the pain slowly vanishes.

"I guess this is love, because it hurts."

Erin laughs boisterously, then pauses as pure elation washes over her. Her mind captures and replays that one special word, a word that has been uttered many a time throughout her life, but a feeling that has been absent for most of it.

With the quickness of a cheetah, she pounces on Bryce, kissing him with a conviction she'd never shown before. Easily kicking off her shoes, she grins back at him.

Like she has so many times, she prepares to reveal herself to Bryce. However, gone is that devilish grin affixed on her face. For the first time in years, she is not partaking in any evil deeds. She knows their mutual passion has meaning beyond satisfying urges and filling bank accounts. As she prepares to strip away Bryce's clothing, she smiles knowing she is finally about to shed her own skin.

Reaching in, Erin lifts Bryce's sweater and undershirt over his head in one fell swoop, prompting his lips to embrace her neck. His hands shift downward, and he tugs her dress up. As Bryce reaches her thighs, she playfully purses her lips and removes his hands.

Gleefully, Erin shakes her head 'no' and grins. She grabs the bottom of her dress herself, bunching it up in her fists. "Allow me," she mouths as she carefully slips her outfit over her head. Bryce's eyes widen and his mouth falls open, ogling the magnificent breasts that are not just his for the night or even for the weekend, but for all-time.

Another fiery kiss follows as Erin frees her hands. Swiftly, Bryce unhooks the front clasp and removes her black bra. He sucks her nipple into his eager mouth as Erin reaches down and undoes his belt. Seeing his cock bulging, desperately begging for freedom, she obliges by unzipping him. Bryce let's her pull away, and she slides his jeans off.

"I've wanted this for so long," she admits as he removes his boxers. " *This*, not... You know. That?"

"Yes!" he confirms.

Protected only by love and desire, Erin prepares to mount Bryce. Then, she pauses and gazes at him for confirmation. Without hesitation, prone and fully hardened, he smiles and nods, affirming his ultimate desire to be one with her.

"Yes," Bryce whispers.

She immediately thrusts herself upon him with delight. Their bodies converge and their souls clash. Heat radiates from their bodies as they move in time.

"Wow!" he bellows.

"Holy fuck!" she responds as she writhes on top of him. "All these years..."

Unable to finish her thought, Erin appears to be in seventh heaven. Blissfully, Bryce marvels at the sight, incapable of comprehending his increased level of pleasure. Their mutual reactions echo the same love language. This is not just sex. It's more. He reaches out for her hand and corrals it. For the first time in their lives, they are making love to their soulmates.

As Erin's gloriously huge tits sway, Bryce's dick twitches feverishly. He holds her hands in his, and her pussy becomes wetter. Every thrust and swivel of her hips draws them both closer to climax.

"I never knew it could be... Oh!... Like this," he pants.

"Oh my God, Bryce!" She whimpers before falling into the throes of ecstasy.

Peering over the edge himself, Bryce tightens his grip on her hips. An incoming explosion, more magnificent than any he's ever known, rapidly approaches. He gasps as his entire body stiffens.

With a familiar yet infinitely more satisfying jolt, Bryce bursts inside of Erin. His love juices fill her sex and propels her over the top as she cums, squirting all over him.

Their bodies are warm and spent, glistening with love, when Erin collapses next to her lover. Satisfied, she reaches over and places her hand on Bryce's racing heart. His hand instantly covers hers as their breathing slows.

Bryce desperately wants to say something poignant. Before this, he would have acknowledged his satisfaction and offered some cool or witty remark. Not this time. No longer confined by an anxiety-riddled need to maintain his stoic façade, he finally blurts out the first thing that pops into his head.

"You have my heart. You always have."

Erin inches her body closer to his and wraps her arms around him, placing her head over his beating chest.

"I'll cherish it always," she says. Then, she lets her eyes close. The room is still as they savor the moment. When Erin opens them again, she flashes him an impish grin and bites her lower lip before asking, "So, what's for dessert?"

Raucous roars erupt from both of them. Bryce wraps his arms around Erin and presses a kiss to the top of her head.

"Cream pie, my dear," Bryce suggests. Erin's eyes dart back and forth between her lover and her pussy.

"Delish!"

"What took us so long?" he wonders.

With a relaxed exhale, Erin echoes the same sentiment. "Oh, Bryce. I'm asking myself the same thing. I've been everywhere and everything I've ever wanted was right here the whole time."

"Should have asked you to prom all those years ago," Bryce muses. He caresses her shoulder blades, then admits. "I was scared for nothing. I should have at least asked you. So stupid."

"I should have looked you up when I got back from Vanderbilt," she replies. "Maybe I wouldn't have wasted my youth on people who only cared about my body."

"I fell in love with you when I was thirteen," he notes.

Cackling, Erin disagrees ever so slightly. "You fell in love with my tits, and you *know* it."

With an earnest, carefree squeeze, Bryce casually objects. "You did it on purpose. You said it yourself. You bent over to give me a show."

"We were just babies. I mean, what do thirteen-year-olds need to fall in love?" Erin asks rhetorically. "Their hearts are in their dicks, or worse, their video games."

Bryce strokes Erin's blackened mane and contemplates her words. As usual, he adds a dash of humor with his retort. "I needed the same thing then as I do now," he reveals. "Truth, passion, heart, a sense of humor... and a nice set of tits."

He then offers a sincere addendum. "Erin, my heart was in my dick for too long. Now, it's in your hands."

She props herself upright and looks at her true love, Solemnly, Erin declares. "And mine is finally in yours where it should have been from the start."

After one more sweet kiss, she slowly stands, grabs her clothes, and briefly retreats to the bathroom. Bryce remains in her bed and closes his eyes, then slowly reopens them. He grabs some tissues, wipes himself off, and waits, listening to the sounds of the faucet turning on and off. When Erin reemerges fully clothed, he exhales and discovers a most amazing phenomenon.

"It really happened," he softly offers. "It wasn't a dream."

"There is one thing I have to tell you," she responds, her tone serious.

Unable to stifle his laughter, Bryce sits up. "Is this the shortest relationship ever?"

"No! God, no!" she quickly answers. "I just... I want to come clean about one thing."

Erin takes a deep breath and summons the courage to tell the truth. "I wasn't out of town that day you came to visit me in Florida. I was scared of meeting you. I mean, yeah, we were old classmates and what-not, but that was twenty-five years ago. I've been burned by plenty of guys, you know?"

Standing up, Bryce approaches her. He keeps his unblinking eyes fixed only on her.

Erin panics. "Please! I should have know—"

But once again, his kiss interrupts her protests.

Erin's anxiety subsides as she melts into his arms. He hugs her tight before pulling back an inch. "All is forgiven," he assures her. "After all, we did have a lovely dinner for two that day. No harm done."

"We sure did!"

Erin strides back into the living room and grabs her phone. From behind, Bryce watches as her fingers scroll with purpose.

"Are you changing your Facebook status already?" he jests.

Smiling wryly, Erin turns towards her newly minted significant other. "No, not yet, but I'll get to it. I'm saying goodbye to my fun Insta," she reveals. "I figure I won't be needing this anymore. I mean, my best client just found himself a girlfriend."

With one last click, Erin says goodbye to her alternate persona. "And it's gone... And here you are. You're not gonna ghost me too, are you?"

Steely determination shines in his eyes as Bryce grabs both of her hands to accentuate his response. "Nope. I'm the man who would cross a thousand oceans, a thousand times over to be with you."

Leaning in, she gently presses a kiss to his forehead. "You're all I have left."

"And you're all I need... But it's my turn to freshen up," he says.

"By all means."

As Bryce does his business, Erin catches a glimpse of the holiday lights illuminating the complex from the patio sliding doors. Her expression of joy slowly fades as she approaches the glass. The longer she stares at the lights, the more forlorn she becomes.

Walking back towards the couch, she almost steps on her guitar lying on the floor. She picks it up, twirls it around, and blows on it for good measure.

"Still mint."

"Thanks," Bryce jokes from behind her. His smirk fades as he catches wind of her concerned visage.

"You alright?"

Inhaling deeply, Erin fights back tears. She points in the general direction of the parking lot.

"Those little trees out there, all lit up for Christmas," she answers. "They make me think of my dad. He's been gone longer than I ever saw him alive."

Comforting her, Bryce places both hands on her upper arms. "I'm sorry."

"It happened senior year at James Monroe," she advises as she proceeds to sit backdown on the couch. "He went golfing one day, and he had this pain in his elbow," Erin begins. "He went to an orthopedist, and they said he was fine. There was nothing broken, nothing torn... Still had the pain though."

Bryce sits down next to her and listens intently.

"They did an x-ray, a biopsy... One thing led to another," she continues. "They said it was, uh, sarcoma of unknown origin."

"Shit. That's terrible."

"Hey, he was a special man," Erin replies. "So special that three doctors got together to review his case, but they all came to the same conclusion. Inoperable. Undetermined primary. Give him steroids to reduce the pain and increase his energy. Start making plans." Erin's voice begins to crack. "He was diagnosed in April, made it to my graduation, and three weeks later, he nosedived. July 28th, he was gone."

Leaning over, Bryce embraces Erin, this time, to comfort her.

Having relived her most painful memory, a despondent Erin cannot help but disclose another hard day not long afterwards. "August 1st. Happy eighteenth birthday, Erin! Time to get packed up to go to college. Time to go out into the real world. You got everything you need? Yeah, sure. Oh, wait. I forgot. My father's..."

Unable to finish her sentence, she breaks down into tears. Erin lets loose, yet she finds a new, unfamiliar calm in Bryce's arms. He gently strokes her back as she sobs into his chest.

"I've never been to therapy," she says, her voice muffled.

"We should go," Bryce answers.

Gradually pulling away, Erin pats Bryce's pecs and wonders, "We? Are we in trouble already?"

"Haha! No, not quite," he replies. "But I, too, know what it's like to lose a parent prematurely. it's been over twenty years since I lost my mother. She was on the plane that hit the Pentagon."

"Oh my God, Bryce!"

"Yeah, she was going out to California to visit my brother," he continues. "Of all the places in the world, Shane had to go to UCLA. Then, he had to stay out there because he found love. That's all fine and good, though."

Bryce's face reveals a moment of clarity as he pauses.

"When it happened, I couldn't be alone. Heather was there. Who would've imagined with her by my side I'd be worse off than being alone?"

Curious, Erin asks, "Where are your dad and your brother, now?"

"Dad died in the line of duty about six months after mom died," Bryce reveals. "Shane just passed away from colon cancer. So, it's just me now... Hey, what about your mom?"

"Huh?" Erin asks.

"Your dad's gone. Is your mom still here?"

Smirking and shaking her head, Erin discloses the sad truth. "Mom didn't approve of me becoming a flight attendant and moving away from home. She and I don't really speak anymore."

"That's unfortunate. I mean, I'm assuming you've tried..."

"Oh, yeah. There's no relationship," Erin confirms. "She's basically disowned me."

Bryce reaches for his discarded beer, then realizes it's lukewarm. "You know, this beer gets warm over time, no matter how cold it is when you first touch it. Maybe?" He lets his words trail off. "I'm just saying."

With a gleam in her eyes, she nods and accepts his thesis for the time being.

"We'll see. Maybe I'll try once more."

Bryce stands and raises his eyebrows. "So, you wanna see *my* hidden talent."

Curious, Erin playfully wobbles in her seat. "You mean there's more? I've witnessed quite a few of them recently."

"Ah, well, this one doesn't involve anything spicy," he advises. "At least, not yet."

Bryce retrieves his phone and opens his Google drive. Then, he hands it over after clicking on his literary work in progress, *How To Die In Roanoke*.

"This doesn't look like anything business-related," she notices as she reads a few lines. "Are you a writer, Mister Br... I mean, Bryce?"

"Hard habit to break, huh?" he jokes as he walks back towards the kitchen. "But yes, I actually published a book last year."

Incredulous, Erin nearly jumps out of her seat. "That's fucking cool!"

Cheerful and confident, Bryce smiles. "You know what else is fucking cool?" he asks.

"Wha—"

He plants one more powerful kiss on her lips, letting his touch linger on the back of her neck. Bryce's answer leaves no doubt where the night, and the rest of their lives, are headed.

"I love you," he proclaims. "That's fucking cool."

"Yes, I'll go to prom with you."

Through ease and unfiltered laughter, the two former classmates-turned-adult lovers enjoy a slew of one-liners, snuggle on the couch, and watch the Washington Capitals game.

Halfway through the first intermission, Bryce receives a Facebook notification.

Erin Gillies tagged you in her relationship status.

"Well, this night can't get any better," Bryce says.

"Ditto," she whispers back.

Bryce and Erin nuzzle, bodies warm and cozy, before gradually drifting into sleep. At long last, they have crossed that bridge.

3) Home of The Amore Special

Into every shining moment a little rain must fall, even on Christmas Eve. Erin knows this all too well. As she sips her morning coffee, she considers Bryce's words. The only family she has left sits in her rocking chair back home in Fredericksburg. They haven't spoken to each other in years.

Figuring she has nothing to lose and everything to gain, Erin sucks up her pride and calls her stubborn, sixty-seven-year-old mother one last time. Her anxiety builds with each ring. Finally, the moment of truth arrives.

Hi. This is Karen. I'm not here right now. Please leave a message. Thank you.

With her heart in her throat and tears welling in her eyes, Erin does her best to leave a coherent message with no hint of heartbreak.

"Hi, Mom. It's Erin. I won't keep you long. I just wanted to wish you a Merry Christmas." She pauses for a moment, searching for what to say. "I, uh... I got a new job at Dulles. I'm not flying anymore, so if you're free tomorrow, I'd..." She swallows hard to wash away her sorrow and finishes her sentence. "I'd love to stop by if you're interested. I'm sure my boyfriend would love to see you, too. Call or text me... Love you , Mom."

Erin deposits her mug in the sink and steps into her bedroom. It's her first PTO day as the Senior Analyst of Distribution and Strategy for Swan Airlines. It's also leg day.

"Navy blue outfit this time," she mutters to herself as she digs her workout attire out of her dresser.

Thirty minutes later, Erin steps through the doors to Red Theory Fitness. The gym is unsurprisingly busy. Everyone is getting their respective reps in before it closes at noon. As she scans her fob, she receives a text. Now more than ever, the name that appears on her screen makes her feel like the luckiest woman on earth.

"Bryce!" she whispers.

Walking towards the leg press, she reads the good news.

> Good morning, Erin! My career may be over, but the Amore Special lives on. My place. Tonight. 6pm.

Beyond thrilled to spend the holiday with her significant other, Erin answers without realizing she's voicing her response out loud.

"Good morning, Bryce. 6pm it is. Are we talking about food or play time, though? LOL."

A familiar sultry voice startles her as she presses send.

"Get it, sis!"

Jumping and turning around, Erin sees her new friend. Her dewy skin glows after another epic workout. She smiles and acknowledges the muscular woman.

"Thanks, Martha," she says as her friend leaves.

Erin continues on and presses one-hundred and fifty pounds thirty times, breaking up the workout in increments of ten. Upon finishing part one of her training session, she finds a new notification on her phone, a simple yet profound response from Bryce.

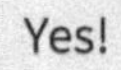

Cooking was never his specialty, yet no one knows better than Bryce how to make his signature creation from scratch. Red snapper, Italian sausage, alfredo sauce, Italian seasoning, and extra virgin olive oil. That, plus the salad with balsamic vinegar and chilled Pinot Grigio, makes for the perfect meal.

Darkness falls on Ashburn as he prepares dinner, yet in Bryce's mind, the sun is shining ever so brightly. He covers the dishes to seal in the warmth. Then, he showers and opts for a distinguished look this evening, the very outfit he wore the first night he and Erin met at the restaurant. Versace La Greca Jacquard blazer. Wide-leg matching pants. A white embroidered shirt neatly pressed.

At ten minutes to six, Bryce's turns the TV on and finds the easy listening music station. He unlocks his front door and leaves it slightly open, just for the thrill of seeing Erin walk through from afar. To enhance the mood, Bryce also dims the lights near the entrance.

Dinner is ready, still simmering quietly as Johnny Mathis croons his own signature number, "Chances Are." When Bryce hears footsteps approaching his condo, he's overcome with a sudden exhilaration, a sensation he has not felt in years. As the distinctive clacking of heels grows louder, his heart beats more rapidly.

The front door swings open. Though Erin's face is hidden, her curves are as prominent as ever. Bryce beams at the sight of his black-haired woman in the entryway, her hands in the pockets of a black overcoat.

"Welcome to Palmieri's!" he announces as he approaches her. "Home of the Amore Special."

As he draws closer to his lady in waiting, Bryce notices her stance. Her silence becomes deafening. Curious, Bryce tries to engage in small talk.

"How was the gym?" he asks.

Without warning, his date shifts, retrieving a cap of pepper spray from the depths of her coat. Her black gloved hand aims and shoots Bryce squarely in the eyes with the offending liquid.

Blinded, Bryce cries out in terrified anguish and stumbles backwards, falling over his coffee table. A familiar laugh echoes throughout his condo, and his heart sinks. He realizes he's in the presence of the devil herself, not his voluptuous angel.

"You should know better than to leave your door unlocked after dark," she insists.

Dramatically tossing her coat, Heather stalks towards Bryce, who is doubled over in agony. In his weakened state, he doesn't notice as she sneaks up behind him. Before he can resist, she applies a chokehold with her right arm, suffocating him while pinning his left arm behind his head.

"I've thought long and hard about doing this to you," Heather states. She forces him to the floor with her, grapevining him with her legs. "But chances are this is lesser of two evils. Either I kill you quickly right now, or she kills you slowly over time."

Bryce flails and screams, trying to break her hold. Pain courses through his reddened face. Heather's heels dig deep into his crotch, exacerbating his utter torture. He bucks his body, but it's futile. Sensing sure victory, her grip only tightens.

"I saw your Facebook status," she taunts. "I figured sex wasn't going to do the trick this time, so I opted for Plan B. You left me with no other choice."

"Heather," he barely eeks out, tapping with his pinned right hand to no avail. "Please..."

"This is what you do to the ones you love," she warns. "And the ones you hate."

Gasping for air, Bryce slumps over and fades rapidly. Imprisoning him against the floor, Heather cackles as her murderous deed nears completion.

"Say hello to Vince and Linda for me," she mockingly requests. "Shane, too. And don't worry about that whore of a girlfriend. She's ne—"

Suddenly, a familiar heavy black scarf wraps around Heather's throat, forcing her to release her death grip. Her eyes bulge in shock and horror as Erin comes to Bryce's rescue.

Grunting and straining with all her might, Bryce's true dark knight yanks on the coarse Mexican serape fabric, squeezing Heather's neck. The scarf grinds against his attacker's skin, digging deep into her throat as Erin doubles her efforts, stepping on Heather's back with her heel.

"Bryce!" Erin screams. "Are you alright?"

Bryce coughs violently and sluggishly crawls out from under Heather, He groans but he's alive. Gagging intensely, Heather flails and pounds on the floor. Erin, fueled by adrenaline, does not relent.

A robust man in uniform rushes through the open front door of Bryce's condo. "Get off her!" he demands of Erin before waist locking her and relieving her of the scarf.

The officer forcibly restrains Erin before Bryce can yell out. "No! Roman, no! She saved me!" The scene before him is a blur of chaos. Barely able to open his eyes or force air through his throat, Bryce points to Heather, expending every bit of his remaining energy to identify the true preparator.

"She tried to kill me," he says before dissolving into a coughing fit.

The officer releases Erin, who scurries behind him and confirms Bryce's claim. "She was choking him out. I had to save him." Peering around Roman, she then looks back at her fallen adversary. Her mouth falls open. Her identity stuns her.

"What the fuck?" she asks, breathlessly. "Martha?"

Dazed, Bryce turns to Erin. "Martha? That's Heather!"

Belligerent, Heather rises to her feet "I'm afraid you're both right," she reveals as she cackles. "All these years, Bryce, and you've never knew the real me."

Like a stone-cold killer, Heather deliberately turns towards Erin.

"And you, Melons, you can't kill me," she insists.

"What the fuck is wrong with you?" Bryce grinds out. Anger pours off of him in waves.

"Ma'am, step away from them and come with me," Officer Roman demands. Duly focused, his hand hovers over his taser. Using the other, he reaches for his radio.

"2-1-7, need backup. Winged Eagle Complex. Unit 316. Suspect female, about 5'11, two hundred, black hair, early forties, highly unstable and aggressive, appears unarmed. 2-1-7, need backup immediately."

"Backup?" Heather scoffs. "Where were they when my father beat the shit out of my mother every night? When he murdered her? I made myself. I built up my body and soul into this impenetrable force. Your *backup* is useless."

Erin crawls over to the bewildered Bryce and holds him in her arms on the floor.

"I've been trying to rid the world of people like that sick fuck," Heather declares, pointing to Erin. "She left him high and dry last year. Don't you remember, Bryce?"

Clutching his throat, Bryce retorts, "*I* decided to come back into her life. I decided. *We* decided. Together! You have a husband and a son, God damnit! What the fuck?"

"Haha. No Bryce. *You* have a son!" Heather reveals. Venom drips from her words. "I saved your ass from having to raise Mikey because Zach is more of a man than you'll ever be. I made you, and I can break you just as easily."

"I don't believe you," Bryce bellows. "You're fucking sick."

"Ma'am, you need help," Officer Roman advises. "Please, come with me, and we'll get you to the right people."

"The right people, Officer Barbrady?" Heather mockingly responds. "The *right people* wouldn't last five minutes with me. Ask Bobby Downing."

Shocked and speechless, Bryce can only mouth the name of his old college teammate.

Seeing the pain on Bryce's face, Erin steps in front of the officer to tell Heather off.

"How *dare* you?" she spits. "Bryce and I love each other! Where the fuck do you get off deciding how to run people's lives? And he has a son? How the fuck did you keep that kind of information from him all these years? You're a heartless psychopath!"

"Oh, please! You're no better than those wretched, expendable men," Heather continues. "You see someone who wants you for your tits. You take his money, and you use him."

"*You* cheated on your husband, and he doesn't even know the kid's not his?" Erin fires back. "*You* introduce yourself to me with a fake name? *You're* a fucking paragon of virtue?"

"Oh, trust me. My life isn't fake. It's all real," Heather replies. "My body's always been good for more than sex. Oh, yeah. Sex sells, but sex also kills. I'm living proof of that."

"Ma'am! Enough!" Officer Roman warns, motioning for Erin to retreat behind him. Erin obliges. "Let's go."

Heather's stubborn, unstable mind refuses to recognize she has been defeated. Furious, she turns her attention to Roman. "You're right, Black Bart. The time for talk is over. I'll take you out first!"

In a fruitless attempt to salvage her ill-fated mission, Heather rushes the officer, who proceeds to tase her. Bryce and Erin watch in utter disbelief as their third wheel convulses and falls helplessly to the floor. Officer Roman closes in and cuffs Heather then turns towards the discarded black overcoat and looks at Erin.

"This yours or hers?" he asks.

Numbly, Erin barely answers, "Hers."

Officer Roman quickly searches her pockets for a weapon, finding an unopened bottle of NyQuil and Heather's wallet with two distinct driver's licenses. Once he's sure she's unarmed, he radios in once again.

"2-1-7, suspect apprehended. Need backup to record victim and witness statements. Winged Eagle Complex. Unit 316. Suspect female. Name is Heather Snow from Ashburn, Virginia. 5'11. Black hair. Age forty-four. Also, please run a check on a Martha Allen from Gallup, New Mexico. Possible lost or stolen identification."

Not a moment later, blurry red and blue lights flash through the window. Bryce regains his footing and stumbles over towards Erin. Immediately, she rushes to him and snatches him into a strong, heart-to-heart embrace.

"I'm so sorry, Erin!" Bryce instinctively says.

"Oh my God, Bryce! I'm so glad you're okay!" she replies, then turns to Roman. "And thank you, Officer! How did you get here so fast?"

"Roman lives three doors down," Bryce softly says.

Breathlessly, Erin chuckles, but before she can reply, Bryce abruptly kisses her. She looks at him, stunned, when he pulls away. "Let's wash out your eyes, hun."

Police rush to the scene of the crime, and a puzzled Officer Roman stares down at Heather, now restrained. After taking a moment to recuperate at the kitchen sink, Bryce and Erin walk back over to them.

"I've known this woman for twenty-five years," Bryce says, studying Heather. "She's always been a little different, but I had no clue she was this psychotic."

Groggy and delirious, Heather turns her head and murmurs.

"I'm sorry, mother. Tell Martha I'm sorry."

Three more officers converge on Heather to take her into custody, but Erin holds up a hand and bends down, leaning in close. "Tell Martha to go fuck herself!" she barks.

Officer Roman chimes in. "Turns out there's no such Martha Allen from Gallup, New Mexico, at least not at the address listed on this *phony* ID. No such license number either. We may have opened up a can of worms with this one."

A strange feeling of calm surges through Bryce and Erin as the police drag Heather away. Then, a familiar burning scent fills his living room.

"Oh, shit!" he exclaims. "Dinner!" Bryce rushes over to his stove to turn off the burners. Smoke cascades through the condo when he lifts the lid off of the pan. In a fitting coda for the evening, his central station fire alarm starts blaring incessantly.

Exhausted, Erin laughs meekly and delivers the most obvious answer for the evening.

"Let's order in tonight."

Bryce nods, and Officer Roman motions for he and Erin to step outside and walk to his apartment to give their statements.

"Oh, I didn't get to tell you," Erin whispers. "We're going to Mom's tomorrow."

As they walk outside and gaze into the drizzly Virginia night, Bryce leans his head against his girlfriend's and uses the last of his remaining resolve to voice his approval.

"Yet another core memory in the making."

4) The Lord of Baltimore

Under normal circumstances, Bryce Palmieri wouldn't care about Edgar Allen Poe's resting place at the famed Westminster Hall. However, his fiancée, Erin Gillies, insists he stop there while visiting downtown Baltimore.

"It's rich with history," she says. "You're an author now, for real. It's a rite of passage. You must do it... And he was my dad's favorite."

Thus, on a mild yet appropriately rainy May morning before Bryce makes his debut appearance at an independent author signing event, he must first pay homage to the master of the macabre. With ample time to spare, he and Erin navigate through the misty streets, arriving at the landmark church and burial ground. The duo turn left onto Greene Street and find curbside parking alongside the massive brick building.

Wet pollen and fallen tree buds line the sidewalk as Bryce cordially guides Erin by the hand down the block and around the corner to the front entrance. The ominous steel Aleko fencing and tan marble and granite tombstones feel strangely inviting. As Bryce walks around the grounds and admires the restored craftsmanship of the cathedral, Erin smiles and gently touches the base of Mr. Poe's grave.

"Hi Dad," she solemnly mutters, imagining him standing there beside her. Before long, Bryce rejoins his lady and motions towards the wooden arches of the front entrance.

"How about a selfie?" he asks.

Despite the way the wind whips her hair around in the breeze, the born-again redhead obliges and snaps the photo for posterity. Captured in a timeless setting, two happy, young souls smile arm in arm for the world to see. Now seventeen months into their relationship, a thousand words are no longer needed to demonstrate how the two forty-six-year-olds have plenty of life left in them.

Before they head back to the car, Erin posts the photo to her personal Instagram, tagging Bryce in the comments.

One disadvantage to living a mere sixty-nine miles away is having to locate a parking garage and wheel books and display accessories in a collapsable wagon four-tenths of a mile to the Lord Baltimore hotel entrance. Alas, that is what the author and his "PA" must do. Neither rain nor distance will deter the man known professionally as Bryce Mayfield from celebrating his first two releases, *Blacksburg Murders* and *How To Die In Roanoke*.

Arriving at yet another landmark structure, this one ripe with dark red brick veneer and limestone trim, Bryce and Erin forge ahead through the busy hotel lobby and into a waiting elevator, which takes them down to the lower level.

The doors open to reveal a reception hall trapped in time. Maroon carpets line the floors, and antique candle holders grace the walls, albeit with electric lights in place of actual wicks. As Bryce and Erin locate the check-in tables, a colonial grandfather clock at the end of the hallway gongs. The pendulum strikes ten.

"Hey there. You must be Bryce," the greeter surmises.

"Um, yeah. Lucky guess, huh?" Bryce notes.

The woman, whose lanyard reads "Brooke", looks back and shrugs awkwardly. An uncomfortable smile follows. "Well, you're, like, one of two male authors here, and the other one already checked in. So..."

"Fair enough," Bryce says. He grabs a gold pen from the linen-covered table and signs the official display sign listing all the attendees.

"So, I'm not the only token peen," he confirms. "That's reassuring."

Brooke laughs heartily as Erin procures his swag bag. With wagon in tow, Bryce and Erin cross into a new realm by entering the gigantic ballroom.

"You know which table we are, right?" he asks, grinning ear to ear.

"Of course, babe!"

As Bryce wanders through the vast sea of books and humanity, Erin is stricken by the French Renaissance architecture and crystal chandeliers.

"Welcome to the Steampunk Era," she jokes.

"Yeah, I think the splatterpunk section is over there," Bryce replies, sarcastically pointing to the back of the room.

Arriving at table sixty-nine, Bryce and Erin meticulously unload their wagon and calmly set up, exactly as they had practiced.

"That was a good idea you had," he notes. "Setting up all this stuff at home first. I swear, I'd be totally lost. Other than this, I *am* totally lost."

"Why?" Erin asks curiously.

Quickly glancing both ways, Bryce leans over to whisper in Erin's ear. "Because I don't belong here," he admits. Saying it out loud makes his chest tighten.

Immediately, Erin puts the brakes on his negativity. She sternly eyes her future husband. "Bryce, look at me!"

When he complies, Erin gently shuts down his imposter syndrome. "You do belong here. Whose name is on the cover of that book, and that one? Huh? *Two* books. *You* did that. This is just the next step. Bryce Mayfield, you belong here! *And* you belong in Roanoke in July. Trust me, when they see that cover and title, they'll eat it up."

After a soothing hug, they finish arranging his table. Bookmarks, stickers, pens, and books are all prominently displayed. Bryce's pedestrian table runner and standing banner are not flashy but they serve their purpose by identifying him as a suspense and thriller author.

With a half hour remaining until VIP entry, Erin activates his square reader for the first time. Still trepidatious, Bryce decides to walk around and get acquainted with his newfound peers to calm his nerves. This also serves as a lowkey way for him to examine other colleagues' table setups and take mental notes for the future.

Amongst a menagerie of mostly dark romance writers, Bryce locates the only other male author in the room, a young spark plug with brown hair who also exudes nervous energy. Particularly taken by his tan Burberry neck warmer, Bryce stops to converse with him.

"I like your scarf," he says.

"Huh?"

"Your scarf," Bryce repeats. "That's quite the attention getter."

Registering Bryce's words through the haze of anxiety, the young man snaps into action. "Oh, yeah! Yeah," he replies, tugging on the fabric. "It's kind of my trademark, you know?"

"My fiancée is a bit of a scarf aficionado herself," advises Bryce, who looks up at the banner that reads *Q.T. McInnis, Romance with A Happy Ending*. He proceeds with an intentional double entendre.

"I believe in happy endings, too," he continues. "I'm Bryce Mayfield."

"Hey, I'm Quinn. Uh, I mean Q.T.," he replies as he shakes Bryce's hand." Sorry, I'm a little nervous. This is my first big signing event."

"Ha! Me too," Bryce responds. "Stick with me, kid. I'm faking it right along with you."

Resting on Q.T.'s table is a stack of his sole paperback offering, a contemporary romance novel titled *Indelible Memories,* along with a collection of character art. Bryce gazes at the male rendering, which looks strikingly similar to Q.T. He then looks at the accompanying female, a sexy, red-haired vixen with wide dimples and enormous tits hidden by a black version of the young author's actual scarf.

"I like your character art," Bryce coyly says.

"Thanks! Yeah, my sister does them. I'm lucky to have her, you know? I'm just starting out. No budget or anything."

"I hear you," Bryce answers, still fixated on the lady portrayed on the 5x7 card. "Sorry, I don't mean to stare. She kinda looks like my significant other."

"Hey, that's cool," Q.T. says. "So, yeah, this is Ellen Black, as in Hell and Back?"

"Nice!"

"Yeah. She's my female main character." He then points to his male main character. "And this one is Jason Summers."

"Let me guess," interrupts Bryce. "Is he chasing Summer?"

Laughing heartily, Q.T. denies any such connection. "No, but that's good. I didn't think of that one. I'm from Florida, so it works."

"Florida, huh?" Bryce responds, briefly harkening back to that glorious day in Orlando when his second chance with Erin began. "I've had some good times down there."

"Haven't we all?" Q.T. jokes. "But, yeah... Not gonna lie, I kinda fashioned Jason as an alter ego of mine. I guess you could say I was inspired."

Bryce smiles since he understands the connection. Reassuringly, he tells Q.T., "Hey, some of the best stories are based on actual events, right?"

"Right?" Curious and desperate to keep the conversation going to relax his own nerves, Q.T. changes the subject. "So, you're engaged, huh?"

"Yup."

"How'd you do it? I mean, how'd you propose? Because I've been seeing someone for about five months now and I'm thinking about it."

Stuffing his hands into his pockets, Bryce lifts his head and recalls the big day.

"It was last June. Erin and I went to her favorite hiking spot, Signal Knob. It's not too far from here — in the northwest part of Virginia."

"Ah, that's cool. You're from Virginia?"

"Yeah, DC area," Bryce answers as he takes in his glorious surroundings. "I'm not exactly the Lord of Baltimore. This is something else."

"I hear you."

"So, anyway, I had the ring in my backpack the whole time," continues Bryce. "We reached the summit. Top of the mountain. She said to me, 'It doesn't get any better than this.' That was my moment. I pulled out the ring and said, 'Oh, yes it does.'"

"That's frickin' awesome! Congrats."

"Thanks!"

His expression suddenly morphs into a quizzical stare. Q.T. confirms Bryce's fiancée's identity. "You said her name was Erin?"

"Yeah."

Bryce refocuses as his counterpart smiles mischievously and looks down at the image on his character art.

"I met a lady named Erin once," Q.T. admits. Then, he pauses and shakes his head, realizing he has omitted the most obvious question of all. "Where are my manners? So, uh, what do you write?"

"Thriller and suspense," confirms Bryce, who gestures back towards Q.T.'s debut novel. "What's this about?"

Swaying back and forth, the young author struggles to answer. "Well, it's kinda like... You ever see the film *The Graduate*?"

"Yeah, not a fan," Bryce replies. "Dustin Hoffman laying around stoned throughout the whole fucking movie? Nah, give me some action, bro."

"Haha! Okay, fair enough, but before that, he scores with the older woman."

Intrigued by Q.T.'s book, Bryce forgoes the young man's awkward attempt at selling and opts to add it to his collection anyway.

"You know what? I'll take one and read the blurb. We gotta work on your elevator pitch."

"My what?"

Laughing and shaking his head, Bryce elaborates. "Think of five key words to sum it all up, something to grab the readers' attention. There's a lot of authors here. If you don't hook them right away, they'll just keep on moving. I watched a bunch of TikTok videos about it. A lot of these seasoned vets give out tips. Very helpful."

"Ah, gotcha."

"How about, uh..." Bryce scans the back of the book. "First love, coming of age," he offers. "Or, how about friends with benefits-turned-lovers? I mean, play with it. See what works for you."

Q.T. suddenly springs to life as Bryce's suggestions strike a chord with him. "Yeah, I like that. I'll use that. Thanks, man!"

"No worries. Listen, I gotta finish setting up. You wanna maybe trade? One of mine for one of yours?"

"Sure, I'll come by in a bit," Q.T. responds. They shake hands again before parting ways for the time being. "Hey, nice to meet you."

"Same here," Bryce says. "Table sixty-nine."

"Nice."

They both chuckle.

Satisfied with having made a new friend, a Bryce uses the restroom and confidently returns to his table. There Erin sits, beaming, before glancing at his new acquisition.

"Q.T. McInnis?" she asks. "Are we adding without subtracting, Mister Bryce?"

Furtively, he looks at his lady who shimmies in her seat. "Dusting off that old chestnut?" he wonders.

"Yeah, that rule no longer applies," she advises. "Aren't you the one who said we leave with less than we came with?"

"I did, and he's coming over here later to take one of mine, *Miss Erin.*"

Bryce's phone abruptly buzzes signaling an incoming text from an unknown number. "Who the fuck is this?" he wonders before reading the message aloud. "Ha! 'Hi Uncle Bryce. It's Mikey. Dad gave me a phone. Tell Aunt Erin I said hi, too.'"

"Aww, that's so cute!" Erin replies, grinning. "Aunt Erin... You know, if I can't be a mom, Aunt Erin is the next best thing."

"For sure. We gotta take Mikey to a Nats game soon."

"Definitely," she agrees. "I'm so glad he likes Britt, though. I'm happy for Zach, too. I think she's a keeper."

"Yeah, what do they say?" Bryce wonders. "Healed hearts heal hearts? Moving from Long Island, starting over. It's the best thing for both of them."

"Yeah. It was so hard for Mikey after, you know, the divorce, and that... Ugh, *person* being in jail. What a fucking psycho!"

"Yup," Bryce responds while shaking his head. "I still can't believe all that shit came out after all those years. What the fuck?"

"Batshit crazy," Erin agrees. She takes in her exquisite surroundings once again. "We should have our wedding here," she jests. "I mean, look at this place."

"I know. It's too late though. We just sent out the invites."

"True," Erin replies. "Hey, my mom asked if we invited my old friend from Vandy. I'm like, 'We haven't spoken in twenty years.' She was like, 'Well, we didn't speak for how long?' I almost liked it better when were weren't talking."

"Ha!" Bryce laughs as he turns towards the ballroom entrance. A crowd has gathered outside the doors. "Looks like they're almost ready."

Quietly reassuring him, Erin peers at her man and gently nods.

"Love you!" she says.

Bryce captures his dream lady in a tender embrace and gently kisses her. "Love you, too!"

Having coasted for years without each other, then conquered life's challenges together, at long last, Bryce and Erin are ready for whatever and whomever walks through that door.

Thank You For Reading

Thank you for reading "Core Memories: The Chronicles of Bryce and Erin" by author Brian Scala. We hope you've enjoyed this tale. Please feel free to leave an honest review on Amazon or Goodreads.

Want more from Brian Scala? Be sure to check out his list of published works and join his newsletter at www.brianscala.com!

Acknowledgements

Thank you to Jennifer Scala for accepting me as an author and for loving me as your husband.

Thank you to my readers, my ARC Team and my Street Team. An author doesn't exist without his or her readers and supporters.

Thank you to Desie and Autumn, Zoe and Sabrina, Shelly, Kitty, Chrissy, AAP, The Hype Girls Squad, and everyone else who has invited me to attend their events as an author.

Thank you to Evie Black, J. Silverton, and Samantha Moran. This book doesn't exist without you. *Dinner For Two* evolved into a real novel thanks to your belief in me. Your friendship helped me push through those bad moments. I'm extremely grateful for all of you.

#DawnRiders!

Also by Brian Scala

Novels:
Being Made (2016)
Eddie The Legend (2023)
Finding Brock (Coming Soon)

The *Core Memories* Short Story Collection:
"Dinner For Two" (2023)
"Sinful Peaks" (2023)
"Black Number One" (2024)
"The Unaliving" (2024)

Additional Short Stories:
"Lust Shack: An *Eddie The Legend* Story":
(Coming October 1st, 2024)

About the Author

Brian Scala is a University of New Haven graduate with a bachelor's in Music Industry. In his free time, he enjoys watching baseball and hockey, finding good burger joints, and traveling to warm weather climates. He resides on Long Island with his loving wife and two American Shorthair cats.

For more information about Brian Scala and his previous works, visit his website at www.brianscala.com .

www.ingramcontent.com/pod-product-compliance
Lightning Source LLC
Chambersburg PA
CBHW032035310726
48972CB00002B/685